Gérard de Villiers

REVENGE OF THE KREMLIN

Gérard de Villiers (1929–2013) is the most popular writer of spy thrillers in French history. His two-hundred-odd books about the adventures of Austrian nobleman and freelance CIA operative Malko Linge have sold millions of copies.

Malko Linge, who first appeared in 1965, has often been compared to Ian Fleming's hero James Bond. The two secret agents share a taste for gunplay and kinky sex, but de Villiers was a journalist at heart, and his books are based on constant travel and reporting in dozens of countries.

On several occasions de Villiers was even ahead of the news. His 1980 novel had Islamists killing President Anwar el-Sādāt of Egypt a year before the event took place. *The Madmen of Benghazi* described CIA involvement in Libya long before the 2012 attack on the Benghazi compound. *Chaos in Kabul* vividly reflected the upheaval in Afghanistan. *Revenge of the Kremlin* lays the assassination of an exiled Russian oligarch in 2013 directly at the feet of President Vladimir Putin.

ALSO BY GÉRARD DE VILLIERS

The Madmen of Benghazi
Chaos in Kabul

REVENGE OF THE KREMLIN

REVENGE

OF THE

KREMLIN

A MALKO LINGE NOVEL

Gérard de Villiers

Translated from the French by William Rodarmor

Vintage Crime/Black Lizard

Vintage Books

A Division of Penguin Random House LLC | New York

A VINTAGE CRIME/BLACK LIZARD ORIGINAL, APRIL 2015

Translation copyright © 2015 by William Rodarmor

All rights reserved. Published in the United States by Vintage Books,
a division of Penguin Random House LLC, New York, and distributed in
Canada by Random House of Canada, a division of Penguin Random House
Ltd., Toronto. Originally published in France as *La vengeance du Kremlin* by
Éditions Gérard de Villiers, Paris, in 2013. Copyright © 2013 by
Éditions Gérard de Villiers.

Vintage is a registered trademark and Vintage Crime/Black Lizard and
colophon are trademarks of Penguin Random House LLC.

The Library of Congress Cataloging-in-Publication Data
Villiers, Gérard de, 1929–2013 author.
[Vengeance du Kremlin. English]
Revenge of the Kremlin : a Malko Linge novel / By Gérard de Villiers ;
Translated from the French by William Rodarmor. — First American Edition.
pages cm — (A Malko Linge novel)
A Vintage Crime/Black Lizard Original
"Originally published in France as La vengeance du Kremlin by Éditions Gérard
de Villiers, Paris, in 2013. Copyright © 2013 by Éditions Gérard de Villiers."
I. Rodarmor, William, editor.   II. Title.
PQ2682 I44 $b V4313 2015   843'.914—dc23   2015004064

Vintage Books Trade Paperback ISBN: 978-0-8041-6935-6
eBook ISBN: 978-0-8041-6936-3

Book design by Joy O'Meara

www.weeklylizard.com

Printed in the United States of America
10   9   8   7   6   5   4   3   2   1

REVENGE OF THE KREMLIN

Moscow
Spring 2013

Rem Tolkachev was so moved, his eyes were moist with tears.

He reread Vladimir Putin's decree, which an orderly had hand-delivered to his little Korpus No. 14 office in the south wing of the Kremlin, for the third time.

The president's order created a special unit within the GRU—the military intelligence service—charged with resolving "sensitive situations." Its members were authorized to travel to any country in the world to secretly kill anyone the Kremlin saw as a political or economic adversary, even if they weren't under official sanction from the Russian government.

It was the return of SMERSH, the organization that assassinated regime opponents in the days of the Soviet Union.

This was a task to which Tolkachev had devoted years of effort, drawing on unlimited resources and the support of Russia's various security agencies. President Putin was now giving official status to his unseen but invaluable role. The old spymaster took no personal pride in this, and he would continue to operate in the shadows, but now he felt imbued with a nearly divine sense of mission.

He mentally blessed Vladimir Vladimirovich, and promised to go to the Cathedral of Christ the Savior to pray for him.

This decree was the final nail in the coffin of the despised Boris Yeltsin, who had dismantled whole swaths of the Soviet Union. Life would now go back to the way it was, thought Tolkachev, with "vertical power" again ruling the country. It would be the USSR without communism, for which no one had any more use. Power would be wielded with an iron fist, and any remaining opponents would soon be brought to heel.

For a few moments, Tolkachev almost felt that his little office shared the solemn mood of the Kremlin's National Security Council hall, with its walls hung with Gobelins tapestries exalting patriotic themes.

Though Tolkachev was one of the most important cogs in the presidential machinery, his office door bore no name. Only its thickness and the sophistication of its digital access lock hinted at its strategic importance. The few people who knew it existed called it Osobié Svyazi, the Office of Special Affairs.

No one could say quite how long Tolkachev had been working there. It was as if he'd been in that wing of the Kremlin forever, and it was almost true. For more than twenty years, the spymaster had obediently followed the orders of all the nation's modern-day czars, from Mikhail Gorbachev to Vladimir Putin.

Born to an NKVD general in Sverdlovsk in 1934, Tolkachev was a classic *silovik*, a person who spent his entire career in the country's intelligence agencies. Gorbachev had brought him into the Kremlin during the reorganization of the Second Directorate of the old KGB, now the FSB—the Federal Security Service. Tolkachev's exemplary personnel file held not the slightest hint of corruption, and he'd shunned the machinations of KGB chief Vladimir Kryuchkov, who was arrested for plotting against Gorbachev.

Not that this meant that Tolkachev approved of Gorbachev's destroying the Soviet Union. In fact, he hated the man. But Tolkachev was too much of a legalist to oppose the country's duly constituted authorities. His mission in the Kremlin was simple: to resolve thorny problems clandestinely and illegally, with the president's support.

The head of state need only mention a problem, without suggesting any particular solution, and Tolkachev would immediately get to work on it.

His heavy, steel-clad file cabinet held the most explosive secrets of two critical periods: the time immediately after communism faded and before the USSR's collapse, and the post-Soviet period, a time of upheaval that saw the collapse of many values established over the previous seventy-five years.

In fact, the cabinet held only a tiny part of the secret operations that Tolkachev had carried out, because most of the instructions he gave were oral. When a written order was required, he hand-typed a single copy on an old Remington manual. He distrusted electronic systems, which he considered too easily penetrated.

Though a man of incredible power, Tolkachev didn't even have a personal secretary. But the head of every civilian and military security service knew they were to obey his orders without question. His name was one of the first ones they were given when they assumed their positions.

His was the voice of the czar.

Tolkachev would be eighty years old soon, but retirement was an alien concept to him, and no one mentioned it. He was practically part of the Kremlin furniture. Besides, who would replace him?

That morning, he had driven his immaculately polished Lada

from his Kastanaevskaya Street apartment in western Moscow into the Kremlin through the Borovitskiy gate. People who passed him in the hallways had no idea how much power was exercised by the little old gentleman with the white hair and unremarkable face.

A widower for the last thirteen years, Tolkachev hardly had any social life. He usually lunched at the Kremlin's Buffet Number 1, where you could get a meal for less than 120 rubles.

People familiar with his office saw further evidence of modesty there. The walls were bare except for a calendar, a photo of Vladimir Putin, and an old poster of Felix Dzerzhinsky, published on his death in 1926. Dzerzhinsky, who created the Cheka, the forerunner of the KGB, was the man Tolkachev most admired in the world. In fact, his few daytime outings were always to the KGB museum on Bolshaya Lubyanka Street, to gaze at his idol's death mask.

Tolkachev's desk was as spartan as his office walls. It had only two telephones and a locked black address book that held the numbers he might need.

One of the phones was connected to the Kremlin's inside system, but Tolkachev's number wasn't listed, and only a handful of people had it. These were usually very high-ranking officials, who were told about Tolkachev when they took their jobs. Most had no idea what he looked like. All they knew of him was his somewhat high-pitched voice with an accent from central Russia.

The armored gray cabinet behind Tolkachev's desk held the files of the people he had used during the last twenty years. They were all there: *siloviki*, crooks, killers, gangsters, priests, and soldiers. Even the dead.

To manipulate these helpers, Tolkachev had unlimited supplies of cash. Packets of bills stood neatly stacked on a cabinet shelf. When he ran low, he wrote a request to the Kremlin administrator. No justification was required, and the money would be delivered the same day. Tolkachev was scrupulously, almost pathologically, honest. He would never take so much as a kopek of the sums at his disposal and kept a meticulous account of the amounts he spent. No one ever asked to see it.

The old spymaster's only pleasure was to serve the *rodina*—the nation—and its incarnation, the president. A special joy, these days, because the current leader symbolized the renewal of the system Tolkachev had dreamed about for years.

Since becoming a widower, he rarely went out, except for a monthly evening at the Bolshoi Theatre, where he paid for his own ticket—he loved the opera—and perhaps dinner in an Italian restaurant on Red Square. When he was under pressure, he chain-smoked slim, pastel-colored Sobranie Cocktail cigarettes, taking eager little puffs as he thought.

Tolkachev's reach was immense. Beneath the shell of a legalist state swarmed parallel services and obscure offices prepared to do anything to help the Kremlin solve its problems. Not to mention all those members of the legal apparatus who were bound to obey the president's representative.

Tolkachev glanced at Putin's order again, this time with a twinge of envy. Russia's master had just made his clandestine role official. But who would be running this new SMERSH? Would he be shunted aside in favor of some GRU general?

It occurred to Tolkachev that his age might be the reason for such a change. Was he considered no longer capable of carrying out his delicate task? If that was the case, he would step aside, as befitted a loyal servant of the state.

Just then a red light started blinking on one of his phones. (Tolkachev felt there was no need for a telephone to have a ringer.) It was the inside Kremlin line. Picking up the phone, he heard a woman's impersonal voice:

"The president wants to see you in his office in half an hour."

She immediately hung up. You didn't question an order from the czar.

Gazing out one of his office windows, Vladimir Putin watched the black birds circling the old fortress and swooping among its golden onion domes. Driven by some mysterious genetic instinct, flocks of crows had been living there for centuries. No one had been able to explain what attracted them to the Kremlin's towers and domes.

Only Boris Yeltsin had ever tried to get rid of them, using trained falcons. A vain effort. The Kremlin crows were still there, and probably would be until the end of time.

Putin was a pragmatic man, and unmoved by the whirling blackness. He wasn't superstitious, either. He glanced at his watch. This was his last meeting of the day. After that he would head to his dacha in Zhukova, a dozen miles west of Moscow, where most of Russia's elite lived. The highway there was supposedly the only one in the country that had no stoplights, so as not to slow official motorcades.

Russia's master was in a very good mood. The work he had begun eight years earlier was nearly finished. He ruled the country with an iron hand, having eliminated practically all his potential opponents. Even marginal groups like Pussy Riot had been put down. Just because you were strong was no reason to show weakness.

Russia itself was doing well, too. Oil and gas brought the state coffers three billion dollars a week, salaries were being paid, the oligarchs cowed, and the security services were fully rebuilt after the 1992 debacle. As in the golden days of the Soviet Union, the people no longer spoke private thoughts aloud.

A hushed voice emerged from his intercom:

"Your visitor is here, Mr. President."

"Show him in."

A few moments later, an unseen hand opened the enormous, leather-lined door. The tiny figure of Rem Tolkachev stood revealed in the entrance.

Putin immediately got up and went to greet his visitor, his hand outstretched. This was a signal honor. The Russian president usually only stood for high-ranking foreign visitors.

"Good afternoon, Rem Stalievitch!" Putin said in his hoarse voice. "Please sit down."

He waved Tolkachev to a long red sofa behind a coffee table with a basket of fruit that nobody ever touched. The president gave his guest a friendly look. One reason he liked Tolkachev was that he was shorter than he was.

Perched on the edge of the sofa, the intimidated spymaster waited to be questioned. Making conversation wasn't up to him.

"Can I assume you are aware of my decree number 27?" Putin began.

Tolkachev nodded cautiously.

"Yes, Mr. President," he said in his squeaky voice.

"What do you think of it?"

The spymaster swallowed.

"I think it's a very wise step, Mr. President."

Putin gave him a long look.

"You didn't feel deprived of any of your prerogatives, I hope?"

Tolkachev stiffened slightly and said:

"I serve the nation and I have always followed orders, sir."

The president gave him an almost affectionate smile. He really did like Tolkachev.

"You would have been wrong to," Putin said dryly. "Because I've decided that you will head the new organization. I didn't include that in my decree, of course; I wanted to tell you personally. I have already informed the GRU leadership."

Tolkachev felt that if he stood up now, his legs might fail him. He had never imagined the president would bestow such an honor on him. It wouldn't change his day-to-day life in any way, but to be officially recognized . . .

"Thank you, sir," he said in a voice heavy with emotion. "Thank you."

Putin brushed the thanks aside and continued:

"I also want to talk to you about another matter. Something that's been on my mind lately."

"What's that, Mr. President?"

"The Berezovsky business. Where are you on that?"

Tolkachev hadn't expected the question and was silent for a few seconds before answering.

"It's been eight years since we've taken any action, per your instructions, sir."

Eight years earlier, the Kremlin had decided to eliminate the oligarch Boris Berezovsky. A member of President Yeltsin's inner circle and former kingmaker, he'd been one of the men behind Putin's rise to power.

Berezovsky, who held a doctorate in mathematics, was working in optimization research when the Soviet Union collapsed. During the period of upheaval that followed, he invested several million dollars in LogoVaz, the country's largest car company. By a series of schemes and scams, he seized control of the company, helped by the Chechen mafia. That turned out to be a dangerous alliance.

In 1993 his Leninsky Prospekt showroom was shot up by gangsters. The following year, he was the target of a Chechen car bomb attack. His driver was decapitated, and Berezovsky barely escaped with his life.

A confused period followed, at the end of which Berezovsky, who had left Moscow for a time, returned and joined the president's "family."

A series of shady deals followed, all struck under Yeltsin's aegis. In those days, Berezovsky could waltz into the president's office at will and shuffle billions of dollars around. In a period of brutal privatizations, he was able to take control of the airline company Aeroflot, the publishing group Kommersant, and the country's biggest television network, ORT.

His masterstroke came in 1995. In association with a partner named Roman Abramovich, he managed to seize control of a huge oil producer, Sibneft. Berezovsky and his associates paid a hundred million dollars for a company that was worth five billion.

He had never ridden so high. A short, balding man with hooded and intense eyes, Berezovsky was at the peak of his glory. In 2000, thanks to his connection with Yeltsin, he helped launch Vladimir Putin as a presidential candidate.

Unfortunately for him, his protégé didn't turn out to be the obedient little *silovik* he expected. From the moment Putin came in power, he single-mindedly starting getting rid of the unscrupulous oligarchs who had ruined the country.

In Russia, nobody stands up to the czar. So most of the oligarchs, including Abramovich, pledged their allegiance to Putin as a way of salvaging part of their fortunes. But Berezovsky resisted. He even counterattacked, suggesting that Putin, to justify war with Chechnya, had orchestrated the 1999 bombings in Moscow that killed hundreds of people and were blamed on the Chechens.

Putin's response was instantaneous.

Following a series of phony trials, the oligarch Mikhail Khodorkovsky was sent to Siberia in 2005. Other oligarchs were ruined and arrested. Fearing the same fate, Berezovsky fled to his French château in Cap d'Antibes. Putin dispatched Abramovich to suggest that Berezovsky give up his share of the ORT network. Otherwise, it would be confiscated.

Russia wasn't a nation of laws, as Berezovsky well knew. He also knew that if he went home, he would be immediately arrested on some pretext and sent to Siberia.

In 2003 he decided to ask Britain for political asylum, and moved to London. He was still very rich, and spent fifty million pounds to settle there with his wife, his mistress, and his six children.

Snubbed by London's high society, he spent most of his time in the Library Bar at the Lanesborough, in the company of the most beautiful Russian prostitutes in London.

He declared open warfare on Putin, and made a series of provocative statements, even threatening a coup d'état. That sealed his fate. Putin hated oligarchs, but he despised traitors.

The final blow to Berezovsky was delivered by his former friend Abramovich. On Putin's orders, he pressured Berezovsky to sell him his share of Sibneft. Berezovsky agreed, and was cheated. Of the agreed 1.4-billion-dollar price, he received only 650 million.

Berezovsky was now in free fall. His Aeroflot deal was but a distant memory, and Putin had gone as far as he could to ruin him financially. Only one task now remained: eliminating him physically.

In 2006, Rem Tolkachev was assigned to carry out a sophisticated, complex operation that would become known as the Litvinenko affair. Alexander Litvinenko was a former FSB agent who fled to London, where he was enlisted by MI5. He was then "turned" by the Russians, who asked him to help kill Berezovsky. A twelve-person FSB team traveled to England with some polonium-210, a substance so radioactive that a few nanograms are enough to cause a horribly painful death.

Litvinenko was still friendly with Berezovsky at the time, and the plan was to poison the oligarch with the polonium. But when Litvinenko met his accomplices at the Millennium Hotel in London, he accidentally drank tea that contained some of the polonium. He wound up at the University College Hospital, where the substance he had ingested was identified shortly before he died.

This clearly pointed to the power behind the incident, because polonium-210 comes only from nuclear reactors, where it is used in tiny doses. Alerted, Scotland Yard went searching for polonium, and found it everywhere: on the seat of a British Airways flight from Moscow to London and on a chair used by one Andrey Lugovoy, an FSB agent. It was also found in Itsu, a Japanese restaurant on Piccadilly, and in the Millennium Hotel. Finally, it turned up in a stadium that hosted an Arsenal–CSKA Moscow football match that Lugovoy had attended.

An immediate hunt for Lugovoy was launched, but he fled London on a Russian Transaero Airlines flight. His accomplices also disappeared.

The British were furious, because Litvinenko had recently been granted British citizenship. The way they saw it, the Russians had come to London to kill one of Britain's own.

From his Kremlin office, Tolkachev supervised the dismantling of the operation, and in the process found the mistake that had given the plot away. The GRU had provided the polonium to the FSB but neglected to explain how to handle it. Tolkachev immediately summoned the GRU general in charge and told him that his lack of oversight had had extremely serious consequences. The English couldn't prove it, but now they knew that the Russians were behind Litvinenko's death.

The GRU general got the message. He went back to his office, took out his 9 mm Makarov, and shot himself. This seemed appropriate. Under Stalin in the Great Patriotic War, Russian generals who lost a battle were executed by firing squad.

After that, things seemed to settle down. Lugovoy became a deputy of the Duma, ignored British extradition demands, and never again left the country. Tolkachev carefully cleaned things up, though he did make another attempt on Berezovsky's life, which failed. The case was then closed.

Temporarily.

Putin broke the long silence.

"I think it's time to reopen that case, Rem Stalievitch. In fact, I opened it myself a few weeks ago."

Tolkachev gaped at him. The master of the Kremlin didn't have to get involved in that sort of thing. That's what he was there for.

An almost joyful light glinted in Putin's light blue eyes.

"I've decided we should take care of that rat Berezovsky," he said. "And this time, I'm sure you'll succeed."

CHAPTER

1

Rem Tolkachev waited for what Vladimir Putin would say next. Intimacy with the president was making him uncomfortable. He didn't have to wait long, because Putin continued.

"We should have reactivated this file earlier, but I wanted to hold off, for political reasons. The British made it clear they were very unhappy about the Litvinenko affair. Fingers were being pointed at us."

The old man opened his mouth to protest, but Putin dismissed any possible objections.

"What's past is past," he said briskly. "Time has passed, and the pressure has eased. My meeting with Prime Minister Cameron last year was encouraging, and it reminded me of an approach I had already thought of. Berezovsky's death must appear to be natural."

"Of course, sir," murmured Tolkachev, though he didn't know quite what the president was getting at.

"In other words, he has to commit suicide," said Putin. "That way, his death won't make any waves in Britain if it's handled properly. And I'm relying on you completely on that point."

"It's an excellent plan, Mr. President," said Tolkachev approvingly.

Putin gave him a smile as cold as ice.

"The prime minister actually gave me the idea, without meaning to. He is proving much more approachable than his predecessor. I think he wants to do a lot of business with us. Without directly raising the Litvinenko affair, Mr. Cameron mentioned that MI5 had reported that Berezovsky was depressed."

"Why?"

"He no longer has much to do, he's lost a lot of money, and he knows he can never go home. I think MI5 has recruited his main bodyguard, Uri Dan, and is getting a lot of their information from him.

"An idea occurred to me at the end of my conversation with Cameron. I mentioned the lawsuit Berezovsky filed against our friend Roman Abramovich. I told the prime minister that it would be helpful if the trial were held quickly, to settle the Sibneft affair. He didn't say anything at the time, but I think he got the message."

Putin went on to describe what happened next.

On August 31, 2012, Boris Berezovsky walked into the London Commercial Court of the High Court, confident of winning his multibillion-dollar lawsuit against Abramovich. He had proof that his former ally had paid him only 650 million dollars for the purchase of Sibneft.

But the judge in the case soon gave the impression of not being completely impartial. In preparing for court, Abramovich paid special attention to his appearance. Though he was the owner of the Chelsea Football Club, he wore an inexpensive watch and modest clothes, and spoke excellent English, quietly. He came across as more British than the queen.

By contrast, Berezovsky loudly proclaimed his rights in broken English, demanding the 4.5 billion dollars he claimed Abramovich still owed him.

A turning point in the trial came when the judge asked Abramovich why he had paid Berezovsky the original 650 million dollars if he had no rights in Sibneft.

"That was for political protection," Abramovich answered. "In those days, Mr. Berezovsky was very close to President Yeltsin."

The judge duly noted the answer, though the argument was so far-fetched it made the Russians in the courtroom smile.

The resulting verdict was a crushing blow for Berezovsky. The judge ruled that he had never owned any shares in Sibneft, and dismissed his claim. Berezovsky left the courtroom visibly shaken. The newspapers later reported that he was depressed.

Putin paused for a moment, then continued in the same quiet voice.

"So that's the foundation I want to build our project on. Suicide is exactly what people would expect from a man who is depressed and bankrupt."

For a moment, Tolkachev didn't dare break the silence. Then he timidly said:

"If that's the case, why not wait for him to really commit suicide?"

Putin shot him a cold, almost hateful look.

"Boris Berezovsky is a rat," he said icily. "Rats never commit suicide. They fight to the death. What we have to do is use the present circumstances to create a setting where suicide becomes plausible. I imagine your disinformation service would be perfect for the task. Then we just act more professionally than we did in the Litvinenko case.

"The whole world must be convinced that Berezovsky really committed suicide. Do you feel capable of handling this two-step operation, Rem Stalievitch?"

"Completely, Mr. President!" said Tolkachev, thrilled to have been confirmed in his position by the president himself.

Putin stood up to signal the end of the interview, and extended his hand.

"Then let's get to work!"

———

Anita Spiridanova was waiting near Leicester Square, looking at the cars coming from Piccadilly Circus. The pretty blonde had tucked her hair under a gray wool cap. Dressed in a down coat, jeans, and boots, she didn't stand out.

Yet she was a very attractive woman and had aroused a flurry of interest at the London School of Business, where she was enrolled for a three-year course before returning to Moscow to work for an import-export company.

A taxi slowly pulled up and stopped. Through the open door Anita saw the smiling face of her boyfriend, a Latvian student named Pyotr Zkatov. She hopped into the taxi, which promptly took off. There was no point in having a car in London. Parking was impossible, and the tow trucks pounced like vultures.

"Where are we going?" she asked.

"To my place in Highgate," said Pyotr, taking her hand.

"Wouldn't you rather go to the Builder's Arms?" she asked hesitantly. "I don't have much time before my meeting."

The young man put his arms around her and pulled her close.

"I haven't seen you for three whole days," he murmured. "Besides, we need to talk."

Glancing up, she melted at the sight of her young lover's gray-blue eyes. The first time they met, Anita had immediately fallen for Pyotr's Baltic charm, his broad shoulders, and his gentle nature. Though Latvian, he was fluent in Russian, and that's what they spoke with each other.

Traffic was snarled, and the taxi crawled along. It was hard to move, even in Bayswater, and then it started to rain. The two young people had stopped talking and were now hugging. Their faces came together in a long kiss. Pyotr discreetly slid his hand under Anita's coat, reaching for her crotch.

At first, he just left his hand there, and Anita seemed to pay it no mind. But then he very gently began to caress her. One of the nice things about London taxis is that behind the window separating customers from the driver, they can do whatever they want—within the somewhat flexible limits of British decency. Pyotr began to feel warmth gradually rising under his palm. Anita shifted backward a little, and he increased his pressure.

He was now stroking her slowly and skillfully.

Anita began to respond, raising her hips against his hand, which molded to her like a second skin. After a little spasm, she brought her mouth close to the young Latvian's ear.

"Stop it!" she murmured. "You're going to make me come."

"No harm in that."

She arched her back.

"But not here! The driver . . ."

Bravely, she pulled away from the hand that was giving her so much pleasure.

The taxi sped up, climbing toward Highgate. Traffic was moving much more smoothly now, and they soon reached the three-story building where Pyotr rented a small flat. The fare came to thirteen pounds.

They bounded up the two flights of old wooden stairs and grabbed each other the moment they were in the apartment, bouncing off the walls. When Anita felt her lover's stiff cock through his pants, she nearly fainted. She stepped back and slid the jeans down his legs, while kicking off her own boots and socks.

For a few moments, the only sounds in the room were the rustling of clothes, and panting. Anita was the more eager of the two. Since they'd started sleeping together a few months earlier, having sex with Pyotr had been a revelation. He wasn't her first lover, but their two bodies felt made for each other.

As soon as she was naked, she flopped down onto the bed on

her back and drew Pyotr to her. He was still wearing his shirt, but Anita didn't care. All she wanted was to have his cock deep inside her. It was like a drug.

He lay on top of her, and she opened her legs, then bent them back and locked them around his hips. Meanwhile, she kissed him deeply, sticking her tongue as far into his mouth as she could.

The young Latvian feverishly slipped his hand between their two bellies, grabbed his cock, and shoved inside her. He was none too gentle, but he knew his partner. When Anita was in this state, she didn't want to be made love to, just fucked, plain and simple. She heaved a deep sigh and squeezed her legs even tighter around her lover's hips.

They were both young, and their coupling was brief. With his cock rubbing hard against her clit, Pyotr soon lost control, shooting his wad into her. And the moment Anita felt that warm, sticky flow, she gave a growl of pleasure and immediately came.

Thighs parted on either side of his legs, she buried her face in his shoulder, her heart pounding, wonderfully happy.

The simple pleasure of a satisfied woman.

She didn't feel like moving and would have happily drifted off to sleep with Pyotr's cock still inside her. But then she remembered that she had a meeting. With great effort, she freed herself from his arms.

"I'm going to have to go," she said with a sigh.

"Wait a minute!" said Pyotr.

"Why?" she asked with a giggle. "Want to do it again?"

"Of course I would. I'd screw you all day long if we had the time. You're the best fuck in London."

Anita didn't much like the phrase, but smiled anyway; it was a compliment, after all.

"As I said, I want to talk to you," he continued.

"What about?"

Pyotr pulled away, and propped himself on one elbow. With his free hand he stroked her breast. Her nipple promptly stiffened.

"Don't do that!" Anita implored him. "It turns me on too much."

"So you like making love with me too?"

Spontaneously, she jumped into his arms and murmured:

"You know I'm crazy about you, crazy about your ..."

Out of modesty, she fell silent.

Pyotr stroked her hair for a moment, then thoughtfully said:

"I'm having a problem with you."

"What's that?"

"I don't want to share you anymore."

To Anita, this felt like being stabbed in the heart.

"But you aren't sharing me!"

"Yes, I am, and you know it. Each time I know that old guy has been fooling around with you it makes me sick and I want us to break up."

Anita was silent for a few seconds.

"I hardly ever see him," she said weakly.

"You see him often enough for him to give you jewelry," he said, pointing to the diamond-studded Patek Philippe watch on her wrist. Berezovsky's birthday present to his mistress had probably cost fifty thousand pounds.

Berezovsky had met Anita when he came to give a speech at her school. They chatted afterward and she had found him fascinating. They wound up being the last people there, and he offered to drive her home. He had a long black Daimler with two bodyguards in front, and a third one behind them on a motorcycle.

Anita knew that Berezovsky was one of the most powerful of the Russian oligarchs, still a billionaire at the time, and in open conflict with Vladimir Putin. After going into exile in London, he had faded from the headlines.

When Berezovsky dropped her off at her Notting Hill flat, she gladly gave him her cell phone number. A short man with a bald head and sloping shoulders, he was far from handsome, but Anita found something magnetic and powerful about his dark, expressive eyes.

He pursued her discreetly, and they went out again. He told her about the complications in his life: separating from his wife, leaving his longtime mistress, problems of all kinds.

One day he invited her to a birthday dinner at the Dorchester, a place she could never have hoped to go on her own. At dessert he brought out a box containing the Patek. She didn't accept it right away, of course; it took a few minutes' discussion. Berezovsky explained that it was nothing for him, costing no more than a week of his bodyguards' salaries. But when he took her hand and said he loved her, Anita felt embarrassed. A man old enough to be her father was declaring his love. They left the Dorchester feeling more intimate, but they didn't have sex that night. Berezovsky merely kissed her, almost chastely, on the corner of her mouth.

He called her often after that, and Anita sometimes accepted an invitation to lunch or dinner. He was still eager and passionate, and she was drawn to the aura of danger that surrounded him. At times, he was pitiable. He claimed she was his only reason for living. He sent her flowers—carnations, in the Russian way. Anita couldn't help but be flattered.

Berezovsky was a powerful, well-known man and very rich. He offered to buy her an apartment, but she had the courage to turn it down.

One day, they arranged to meet at his office on Down Street, off Piccadilly, at six in the evening. When he opened the door himself, Anita realized that the staff had gone home.

In the big conference room, he became passionate. He shoved her against the big maple table, pawing at her clothes, saying how much he wanted her. Though it felt cowardly, she yielded. They made love, but she didn't particularly enjoy it. It was a kind of formality.

Berezovsky, on the other hand, was in seventh heaven. The next day she received a parcel from him that contained the kind of Chanel suit she had always dreamed of.

At the time, she promised herself that it wouldn't happen again. But he was so eager and so much in love that she gave in from time to time, out of weariness. One day in the *Daily Mirror* she saw a photo of them arm in arm, coming out of the Connaught on Carlos Place. The caption mentioned the Russian oligarch's new young girlfriend, without giving her name.

A furious Pyotr phoned her within the hour.

The conversation was angry, and they didn't see each other for ten days. She was the one to finally phone. He agreed to see her, and they made love.

She promised she would never see Berezovsky again, but didn't keep her word. The stooped figure of the oligarch had hung between them ever since.

Occasionally when Pyotr asked her to dinner and she turned him down, he immediately knew whom she had a date with.

They hadn't mentioned it again, until today.

Catching her eye, Pyotr spoke somberly.

"This business has been eating at me for a long time," he said. "I know you see him regularly, and you shag him."

"I hate that word!" she protested.

"Too bad. I've thought it over. Here's the deal: you have to choose between us."

"Pyotr! It's you I'm in love with, not him!"

The young man glowered at her.

"But you still drop your knickers for him."

Anita was silent. Pyotr had started putting his clothes back on, and she had a sudden moment of panic.

"I won't see him anymore! I swear!"

"You said that before, and I don't believe it. The old man mesmerizes you."

Pyotr had just pulled on his T-shirt, and the sight of his abs rippling under the fabric rattled her. She didn't want to lose him.

"What do you want me to do?"

"That's your business," snapped the young Latvian. "But I'm done sharing you."

"All right. I'll tell him I don't want to see him anymore."

Pyotr shook his head, then said:

"Do it right now."

"How?"

"Send him a text. One that's perfectly clear."

Anita hesitated only a few moments. Taking out her cell, she drafted a quick text, then held the phone out to him.

"How's this?"

It was very brief:

I don't want to see you anymore, Boris. I don't love you. Don't try to contact me. Good luck. Anita.

"So, what do you think?" she asked, somewhat sharply.

"It's okay. But you better keep your promise."

"I will."

She hit "Send," and when the text had been sent, she felt a twinge of regret. But the sensation of having Pyotr's prick deep in her cunt was too strong for her to regret her decision.

She stood up, and Pyotr hugged her very tightly.

"Now we'll really love each other," he said.

Four days had passed since Anita's breakup message, and she hadn't heard anything from Berezovsky. Walking to the Tube, she saw the current issue of *Closer* on a newsstand and was shocked to see a photograph of herself splashed across the cover, though her face was blurred.

The headline was explicit:

"Boris Berezovsky's young lover calls it off!"

Anita bought a copy of the magazine and read the article on the Tube. It didn't give any details about their breakup, but Berezovsky was said to have complained bitterly to friends that he'd been ditched by a young girlfriend he loved very much. The writer said that the friends thought the breakup had greatly affected his mood, and that he no longer wanted to see anybody. Anita wondered how the information had gotten to *Closer*, but couldn't come up with an answer.

At least Pyotr will be happy, she thought. For now, that was all that mattered.

CHAPTER

2

"Sir, the gentleman on the line has called several times since yesterday, and he insists on talking to you."

Berezovsky's Israeli bodyguard had politely approached his boss, who was in his office reading the *Times*.

The oligarch glanced up.

"What does he want?"

"He says you know him," said Uri Dan. "His name is Ilya Sokolov, and he writes for *Forbes Russia*."

The journalist had called on the mansion's landline phone. Since selling his own house, Berezovsky was living at his ex-wife's property in Sunningdale. It was near Ascot in Berkshire, about thirty miles west of London. He had withdrawn from public life in the last few months. He gave up his Piccadilly office, let three of his four bodyguards go—keeping only Uri Dan—and went out only on personal business.

Berezovsky hesitated.

Forbes Russia was in the hands of people close to the Kremlin. A few months earlier the magazine had run a nasty article calling him a criminal and dubbing him "the Kremlin Godfather." He had sued for libel, of course, but the case was now mired in the shifting sands of Russian justice.

"Tell him I'm not here."

27

"He'll just call back," said Dan. "He said he was leaving for Moscow tomorrow morning and really wanted to talk to you first."

Berezovsky hesitated again. He had promised the British authorities that he wouldn't talk to the press while his appeal of the Abramovich verdict was pending. On the other hand, he was intrigued by the request from this Russian journalist, about whom he knew nothing.

"Give me the phone."

Dan handed him the telephone.

"*Shto vui hatite*?" What do you want? asked Berezovsky.

What a relief to be speaking Russian, he thought. In Britain, Berezovsky insisted on speaking English, even though he hadn't mastered it. This had hurt him in his suit against Abramovich. He felt sure he'd been adopted by the British, but in fact he wasn't.

"I absolutely have to meet you, Gospodin Berezovsky," said Sokolov. "I feel you've been treated unfairly, and I'd like to set the record straight on a number of points. Can I call on you at your home?"

"No, I never see visitors here."

The conversation continued, with the journalist becoming increasingly insistent. Finally, Berezovsky gave in.

"All right, I'll meet you at the Four Seasons bar at five o'clock this evening."

He was going up to London anyway, for a dinner date with a young Russian woman he'd met. In her company, maybe he would be able to forget his beloved Anita Spiridanova.

Berezovsky hung up and called his bodyguard.

"We're leaving for London at four o'clock, Uri."

It was Friday, but the inbound traffic wouldn't be too bad. Since laying off his other bodyguards, he used Dan as his driver. Scotland Yard, which had once provided security for him, no longer escorted the black Daimler. Berezovsky had been left to his own devices, but didn't feel in any danger. He hadn't received any threats, direct or indirect, since the Litvinenko affair, though he knew that Vladimir Putin's hatred for him was as strong as ever.

Dan clicked the remote, opening the estate gate, and drove up the driveway to the house. He had gone out just before lunch to run some errands in London for Berezovsky, leaving him alone in the house.

It was Saturday, and the housekeeper-cook wouldn't arrive until later in the afternoon.

Since leaving his mistress Elena Gorbunova the previous December, Berezovsky had lived alone. He occasionally spent whole days without leaving the estate, just reading or making phone calls. He was still active, however. He had many friends in Israel, a country where he felt safe, and planned to fly there on the following Monday. His old friend Michael Cherney had reserved him a room at the Dan Tel Aviv.

At first, Dan was surprised not to see Berezovsky. His boss never went out alone, so he figured he must be somewhere in the house.

Just then his phone rang. It was Lisa, one of Berezovsky's daughters, who was very close to her father.

"I can't reach Papa," she said. "He's not answering his cell. Would you try to find him? Have him call me!"

Dan hung up and went looking for his boss.

Berezovsky was neither in his bedroom nor in his office. After going through the house, Dan stopped at the master bathroom and noticed that the door was locked. That was odd. Berezovsky wasn't in the habit of taking a bath at that hour. Intrigued, he knocked on the door, but got no answer.

Dan knocked louder, but with no more result. Now quite worried, he decided to break it down. Maybe Berezovsky had fainted. . . .

Smashing the door open, Dan burst into the bathroom, only to stop at the sight of the body on the tiled floor.

The oligarch was lying on his side, fully dressed, with a length of cord around his neck. The other end was dangling from the showerhead. He had apparently locked the door so as not to be disturbed, and hanged himself. He wasn't breathing.

Dan immediately called the local police, then Lisa, the daughter who'd tried to reach him earlier. The reason Berezovsky hadn't answered his cell was now obvious.

The CIA occupied the fourth floor of the American embassy in London, and Stanley Dexter had a beautiful view over the trees in Grosvenor Square. He had replaced Richard Spicer as London CIA station chief when Spicer went back to Washington.

Dexter's secretary ushered Malko Linge into the office.

The Vienna CIA station chief had asked Malko to fly to London, without saying why. They had reserved him a room at the Lanesborough on Hyde Park Corner, and he'd taken a taxi to the appointment.

Dexter came forward to meet him, hand outstretched. "It's nice to meet at last, Malko. Richard told me a lot about you. I gather you and he worked on a number of cases together."

"That's right."

Dexter turned out to be an old CIA hand near the end of his career. He was very slim, with glasses and a well-trimmed goatee, and eyes that sparkled with intelligence.

As the two men chatted, Malko knew they wouldn't get to the heart of the matter right away.

"Can I take you to lunch?" asked Dexter affably. "I've reserved us a table at the Dorchester."

They talked for a little while longer, then went down to the underground garage to get Dexter's Ford.

The Dorchester dining room was crowded, but they were given a circular booth in the center of the room that was far enough from the other tables to allow for discreet conversation.

After ordering, Dexter looked at Malko with a slight smile.

"I assume you're aware of Boris Berezovsky's death," he said.

"I know what the newspapers wrote about it," said Malko. "I was in Vienna when he died."

Three weeks earlier, Berezovsky's bodyguard had found the oligarch dead in his bathroom. A few days ago, he had been buried at Brookwood Cemetery in Surrey. The funeral was attended by only about thirty people, most of them family.

The British press didn't give the death much coverage, beyond noting the claims by some of Berezovsky's friends that he'd been killed by Russian intelligence.

"What do you think about it?" Dexter asked as they were served shrimp and avocado salad.

"I don't really know what to think," said Malko. "The British police seem inclined to call it suicide."

"It was the local police that did the investigation," the CIA station chief pointed out. "They just went by appearances. Besides, the forensic lab results aren't available yet."

"Any sign of someone entering from the outside?"

"None," said Dexter. "Berezovsky was found lying on the bathroom floor, apparently having hanged himself. There were no witnesses. He lived alone and his bodyguard had been away for several hours, running errands for him."

"And he didn't leave a note?"

"No, nothing."

"What is the family saying?" asked Malko.

"Not much. His daughter Lisa has been almost totally silent. But his close friends think he was killed on orders from the Kremlin. Vladimir Putin's revenge."

"Anything's possible," said Malko. "After all my years working against the Russians, I ought to know. The Kremlin tried to kill Berezovsky eight years ago with polonium-210."

"I read your report, and I discussed it with our friends in MI5," said Dexter. "Like you, they're positive the polonium wasn't destined for Litvinenko, but Berezovsky. A mistake in handling it caused Litvinenko's death. But the Moscow killers got out of England without being arrested, so the Brits can't be sure. Let me repeat my question. What do *you* think of the suicide theory?"

"I don't have any evidence to refute it," said Malko carefully. "But I met Berezovsky a couple of times, and he didn't seem like the kind of man to commit suicide."

"That's what his friends say. They're all sure he was killed."

"And what do *you* think, Stanley?"

"I share their opinion," he said quietly. "And that's why you're here in London."

The mood in the quiet dining room abruptly shifted. Malko knew that the London CIA station chief wasn't talking casually.

Just then, a waiter served Malko a mouth-watering slice of roast beef, that great British specialty. After he left, Malko asked:

"What led you to that conclusion?"

"An accumulation of evidence. Here at the station, we've followed developments in the Litvinenko case, even though it doesn't directly concern us. A topic you know well."

"I was always convinced that the real target was Berezovsky," said Malko. "What happened later at the Lanesborough bar proved me right."

Dexter said:

"As you know, we pay close attention to what the Russian intelligence agencies do abroad. Washington feels the Cold War has started up again, in a more low-key way. Fact is, Vladimir Putin hates our guts. We used to keep an eye on Berezovsky because he knew a lot about Putin that might have interested us. Now it's too late."

"Did you ever try to talk to him?" asked Malko.

"He refused any contact with us; too anxious. Anyway, MI5 was protecting him in those days. We figured we had plenty of time."

"So why do you think Berezovsky was killed?" asked Malko again.

The station chief answered the question with one of his own.

"Do you remember the KGB's disinformation service?"

"Sure. They launched the big public manipulation operations, like the Stockholm Appeal. They used the people that Lenin called useful idiots."

"Well, the KGB is gone but the disinformation department still exists," said Dexter. "Only now it's run directly by the Kremlin and not the SVR"—the Russian foreign intelligence agency. "Its mission is to minimize negative news and discredit any coverage that makes Russia look bad."

"Why do you mention it?"

"You remember Berezovsky's lawsuit against his former partner Roman Abramovich, don't you?"

"Of course. Berezovsky lost the case."

"Under very strange circumstances," said Dexter. "The trial was supposed to be held in October 2012, but the date was moved up by two months, and the verdict delivered on August 31. The judge ruled against Berezovsky, denying that he had any rights in Sib-neft."

"It was a court decision," said Malko. "These things happen."

"Sure, but there are two troublesome facts. First, Putin came to London to visit Cameron shortly before the trial. The British press noted their shared outlook for the future of Russo-British business relationships.

"Then the judge in the Berezovsky case behaved in a way that seemed oddly hostile to him. She treated him contemptuously, refused to hear him out, and didn't give enough weight to the evidence he presented. It was as if someone had gotten to her."

"So what do you conclude from this?" asked Malko.

"We don't have any proof, of course, but we suspect a political deal was struck between Putin and Cameron. Unlike his predecessor, the prime minister has been much more receptive to Russian positions. The previous government moved heaven and earth to find Litvinenko's killers. It even identified two FSB agents who brought the polonium to England.

"The media revealed that Alexander Litvinenko had become a British citizen with ties to MI5. In other words, the Russians had come to England to kill a Brit. A very messy situation."

"And you think the Berezovsky verdict was the result of pressure?"

"It's not out of the question," said Dexter. "The case didn't make a big public splash. But the coincidence is disturbing. Putin visits London, the trial is moved up, and Berezovsky loses it when he should have won."

"I can understand Putin's interest, since he hated Berezovsky," said Malko. "But what's in it for David Cameron?"

"I can think of three things," said the station chief. "One: Cameron is on the outs with China for having met with the Dalai Lama, and he might hope Putin would smooth things over. Two: Britain reached an agreement with Russia to help with security at the Sochi Olympics. And three: Cameron wants to increase British exports to Russia.

"The Litvinenko case is seven years old now, and it doesn't carry much weight in matters of state. And while it was true that Litvinenko was a British citizen, he'd become one only recently."

A hush descended on the two men. All British citizens are equal, but some are less equal than others, apparently.

"All right," said Malko. "Let's say Cameron wants to bury the hatchet with the Russians for political reasons. What do the Russians get out of this?"

Dexter put down his fork, looking serious.

"Here's my theory," he said. "The Russians are chess players. They plan their moves ahead. Putin still wants to kill Berezovsky, but in light of his new relationship with England, he knows he can't act as brutally as in the Litvinenko case. So he starts laying the groundwork.

"After the Abramovich verdict, our Moscow station forwarded to us a lot of media reports that said Berezovsky was bankrupt and depressed and was thinking of killing himself. By a funny coincidence, those articles all appeared in publications controlled by the Kremlin. Some were picked up verbatim by the British press, describing Berezovsky as a ruined man. As I see it, that was the first stage of the operation."

"What do you mean?" asked Malko.

Dexter looked at him seriously.

"To keep Berezovsky's death from making waves, the suicide thesis has to appear plausible. How you do that? By spreading the notion that he was depressed and thinking of ending it all."

"That's a very big deal!" exclaimed Malko. "You're suggesting that Vladimir Putin and David Cameron conspired to make Berezovsky's suicide believable."

"It's even more complicated than that," said the CIA station chief. "I have evidence that suggests Putin took Cameron for a ride."

"Cameron decided to make peace with Putin by dropping the Litvinenko case, which wasn't going anywhere anyway," said Dexter. "But I don't think he imagined just how diabolical the Kremlin's plot was.

"After the Abramovich trial, a slew of articles about Berezovsky's financial and personal difficulties started coming out. Before he died, for example, the tabloids trumpeted his split from a young Russian woman named Anita Spiridanova, saying it had broken his heart."

"Who is she?" asked Malko

"A business student here in London," said Dexter. "MI5 learned that she also had another lover besides Berezovsky, a good-looking Latvian boy we don't know much about. The guy's name is Pyotr Zkatov, and we've asked our Riga station to check him out."

"How did the newspapers hear about the breakup?"

"We don't know, and we're trying to find out. And here's something else. The evening before his death, Berezovsky met with a Russian journalist from *Forbes Russia* at the Four Seasons. The magazine is part of the Kommersant group that Berezovsky once owned, but is now controlled by the Kremlin. The journalist's name is Ilya Sokolov.

"Nobody knows what they talked about, but soon after

Berezovsky's death, Sokolov wrote a story in the magazine quoting him as saying he had lost his will to live after his financial reverses. In the same article, Sokolov claimed Berezovsky let his bodyguards go because he couldn't pay them. Couldn't pay his legal bills, either."

"Pretty disturbing," said Malko.

"But here's the kicker," said Dexter. "The next day, the Kremlin published a communiqué stating that Berezovsky had written to Putin for permission to return to Russia, saying he couldn't stand living in England anymore."

"Did they publish the letter?"

Dexter smiled cynically.

"No, but they're very good at forging documents. At Nuremberg the Soviets tried to introduce phony documents into evidence that exonerated them from killing those Polish officers in the Katyn Forest massacre.

"In other words, the Russians did everything in their power to spread the idea that Berezovsky was at the end of his rope, bankrupt, and tired of living. At that point, all they had to do was send in a kill team. That's another thing they're good at, but we can talk about that later."

Malko was silent. If what Dexter was saying was true, it was an extremely clever operation. And the CIA station chief's version of the situation explained a lot.

Just then, the waiter brought the two men some strawberry tarts that were so beautiful, they belonged under glass.

"Of course all this is just a theory," said Malko, playing devil's advocate. "Too bad there's nothing concrete behind it."

"Actually, there is," said Dexter dryly. "I've been able to establish at least one thing. Berezovsky may had lost most of his fortune, but he sure wasn't bankrupt. By the end of the summer, he was due to acquire the assets of two investment funds totaling 650 million dollars. Besides, he had extensive real estate holdings and lots of money in Israel."

"He could be rich and still want to kill himself," Malko pointed out.

"That's true," said Dexter. "But here's another curious fact. On Friday, the evening before his so-called suicide, he booked a ticket for Tel Aviv for the following Monday. He was to meet one of his friends, Michael Cherney, and spend a week vacationing with another of his Russian girlfriends."

The two men dug into their strawberry tarts in silence. The more Malko thought about it, the more he could imagine Putin killing Berezovsky to settle an old score. As he'd said earlier, he couldn't see the oligarch committing suicide; it wasn't in his DNA. Malko was inclined to agree that Dexter was right, but one thing still puzzled him.

"Stanley, we're in London, the so-called suicide happened in Surrey, and Berezovsky was being protected by MI5. Why are you involved in all this?"

"That's a good question," Dexter admitted, setting his dessert fork down. "Normally, I wouldn't have asked you to come here, and gone to see my MI5 counterpart instead. But there's a hitch.

"The foreign secretary just asked the judge on the Litvinenko case—which is still open—not to reveal any classified information that reflects badly on Moscow. In the name of national security. Sir Robert Owen, the coroner, was very unhappy with the request. He said this forced him to record an open verdict, which would be incomplete, inaccurate, and unfair. But he obeyed. In practical terms, this means the whole thing is classified."

Malko was astonished.

"Why in the world would the British take such an unusual step?"

Dexter smiled thinly.

"Let's just say that it happened after Cameron made a trip to Sochi, where he met with Putin. The Russians and the British must have signed a secret intelligence accord. For the Brits, the price was dropping the Litvinenko case. They might also be trying to get Moscow's help in dealing with Syria."

Malko was still dubious.

"Litvinenko is dead and buried, but now Berezovsky has died," he said. "Didn't you discuss that with your colleagues at MI5?"

"Of course I did, and it made them very uncomfortable. The investigation was handled by the local police, who haven't released their findings. They concluded that it was a suicide.

"When I met with the head of MI5, he tried to convince me that he subscribed to the suicide theory, but I got the feeling he'd been ordered to hush up the affair. So Berezovsky's in the ground and the whole business will gradually be forgotten."

"It's very strange to imagine British intelligence knuckling under to the FSB," said Malko.

Dexter sighed.

"That's the price of the rapprochement with the Russians. I'm sure the PM feels that his country's interests require sacrificing Berezovsky. The British have never been sentimental. And after all, he was just another political refugee with a shady past."

"So as far as the British are concerned, the case is closed," said Malko.

"I'm afraid so, unless something pops up. The courts and the police have been given their marching orders. Even if the opposition protests, it won't change anything."

Malko finished his coffee and ordered a refill.

"If that's the situation, why summon me to London?"

"The order came from Langley, which is very worried by this rapprochement with the Russians. British intelligence was deeply penetrated by the Russians in the old days. Remember the Cambridge Five affair in the 1950s, with Maclean and Burgess? Things got so bad, we stopped sharing actionable intelligence with them. We don't want that to happen again.

"Besides, we'd like to know how extensive the Russian networks in London are. Killing Berezovsky would have required a lot of people, a big operation. Bigger than for Litvinenko. So the more we know about that, the better. Don't forget, the Russians are still our number one adversary."

"Who will you name to carry out the investigation?"

The station chief smiled at Malko innocently.

"You," he said.

The silence that followed was broken only by the hushed conversations in the dining room.

Dexter continued:

"After talking with the MI5 people, I decided I couldn't count on them," he said. "They'll put up a smoke screen. I didn't even mention your name."

"But they must be aware I'm in London," objected Malko. "They still know how to do their job."

"Of course, but I doubt they'll get in your way. I think we can expect them to remain neutral. Possibly helpful, but certainly not hostile."

The old days of cooperation between the two intelligence services were long gone, Malko reflected. He still remembered pleasant dinners at the Travellers Club with Sir William Wolseley, chief of staff to the then director general of MI5. Now he was practically undercover in England, the country that was supposedly America's best ally.

"I'm flattered at the Agency's confidence in me, but what can I do?"

"You knew the Litvinenko affair protagonists, you speak Russian, and you knew Berezovsky."

"That's all true, but where do I start?"

"As I see it, there's an invaluable witness in the case: Uri Dan, the bodyguard who found Berezovsky. Along with the local police, he's the only person who actually saw the scene."

Dexter paused, then continued.

"We don't even know if there was a chair or a stool in the bathroom, Malko! Usually when you hang yourself, you step onto something and you jump. Here, nobody mentioned a stool. Which means that Berezovsky tied the rope to the showerhead and let himself fall. The rope snapped, so he shouldn't even be dead. Not even a four-year-old would believe that story."

"And the British aren't saying anything about this?" asked Malko.

"MI5 claims the local police haven't spoken to them."

"So where is this bodyguard, Uri Dan?"

"We don't know," Dexter admitted. "We don't even know if he's still in the U.K. He was living with Berezovsky, and the house is under seal. If I ask the Brits, they'll clam up, so we have to find him ourselves."

"How?" asked Malko.

"One of Berezovsky's friends might know," said Dexter. "A man named Nikolai Glushkov. They'd known each other since 1989 and met again in London after Glushkov spent three and a half years in a Moscow prison over some shady financial dealings. He was one of the people who told the papers that Berezovsky had been killed, so I think he'll cooperate."

"Do you know him?" asked Malko.

"No, but we have his cell number. I suggest you call and tell him who you are. Glushkov can lead you to Uri Dan, who's the key person, as far as I'm concerned."

"Any chance Dan could have been an accomplice?"

"I don't have a feeling either way," said Dexter. "He's Israeli, but that doesn't mean anything. But he knows what shape Berezovsky was in, in that bathroom."

"So that's all of it?"

"No, of course not," said Dexter, signaling for the check. "I have a whole file on this. I'll bring you up to speed back at my office. A lot of strange people were hanging around Berezovsky."

Leaving the Dorchester in Dexter's Ford, Malko felt both perplexed and intrigued. The conversation brought him back seven years. In his mind's eye, he could still see a cadaverous Alexander Litvinenko on his hospital bed, claiming that he'd been killed by the KGB. He died the following day.

Except that back then, Malko had the support of the British authorities. Now he found himself alone, facing a Russia as shadowy and dangerous as ever.

In the car, he asked Dexter:

"Do you know Gwyneth Robertson?"

The CIA man smiled.

"I've heard of her, but she'd already left the Agency when I got to London. She was a very good case officer, and we were sorry to lose her. Some think tank offered her so much money she couldn't refuse. I see in your 201 file that you two worked together a few times."

"That's right," said Malko, without elaborating.

The delicious Gwyneth Robertson was no longer with the CIA and was rolling in money, but she was probably still the exciting slut he'd known. If she was still in London, she might keep him from getting too lonely.

"Malko!" she cried. "Are you in town?"

"I got here yesterday. Do you still remember me?"

Gwyneth gave a throaty laugh. "You're one of those people you don't forget. Besides, we had a lot of fun together."

"Are you still working hard?"

"Yes, and I'm making more money than ever!" she said. "Let me take you to dinner. Where are you staying?"

"At the Lanesborough."

"Cool. I'll pick you up at eight."

It was six o'clock, so Malko had time to get some rest. And do some work.

When Malko called Glushkov, the phone rang for so long that he was about to hang up when a man with a very deep voice finally answered.

"Nikolai Glushkov?" asked Malko.

"*Da.*"

"*Dobriy vecher,*" he said. Malko continued in Russian. "You don't know me, but it might be useful for us to meet."

In a few words, he explained what he was doing in London, and why. Glushkov listened without interrupting. Malko concluded by saying:

"I'd like to hear what you think about the death of your friend Boris Berezovsky."

"Who are you working for?" Glushkov asked after a pause.

"I will tell you if and when we meet."

"The British?" A touch of asperity.

"No. But I know the Litvinenko case well. I was here seven years ago, when he died."

"All right, I'll meet with you. Where are you staying?"

"At the Lanesborough."

"There are too many Russians there. I'd rather meet you at the bar at the Hilton. I'm busy right now, so let's say two days from now, at six o'clock."

———

Malko was lounging in one of the red velvet armchairs of the Lanesborough's Library Bar and sipping a Russky Standart when Gwyneth Robertson came in. She was wearing a tailored tweed suit with a daringly short skirt. When she flopped down next to Malko, she crossed her legs high enough to give him a brief glimpse of a garter. Though American, she had perfectly mastered the codes of European eroticism.

"You haven't changed," she said, giving Malko a meaningful look.

"Champagne?"

She shook her head.

"No, thanks, I'm starving. Come along!"

He polished off his vodka and followed her, saluted by the doorman, who opened the door of a beautiful gray Bentley coupe for them. The days when Gwyneth tooled around in a Mini Cooper were clearly long gone. She smiled at Malko's look of amusement.

"I just got another raise," she said. "It seems my analyses have earned a lot of money for one of our clients, and they gave me a bonus of five hundred thousand pounds. So I treated myself."

She slipped behind the wheel, and they took off.

"Where are we going?" he asked.

"To a very 'in' place, Masala on Tottenham Court Road. The food's delicious, and the place isn't expensive, but you have to reserve a year in advance. If you're five minutes late, you don't get a table."

As the Bentley merged with the fast-moving traffic, Malko leaned back, enjoying the car's heady smell of new leather.

At a red light, Gwyneth turned to him.

"Since you're not doing anything, why don't you pay me some attention?" she said playfully. "We still have quite a ways to go."

When the light turned green, Malko put his hand under her

tweed skirt and moved up her stocking and garter belt until he reached bare skin.

Soft and warm.

Pressing on, he reached some tiny nylon panties and began to stroke them. Gwyneth purred with pleasure, and they didn't exchange another word until they got to the restaurant, where she left the Bentley with a valet. The dining room was jammed, but a dewy-eyed young man waved in greeting and led them to a minuscule table.

"You naughty girl!" he exclaimed. "A minute longer, and I couldn't hold the table for you."

Gwyneth ordered a bottle of Château Pétrus the moment she sat down, clearly determined to burn through her bonus. She and Malko clinked glasses.

"They finally got him this time," she said with a half smile.

No need to ask who she was talking about.

"Do you know anything?"

She shook her head.

"No, I'm out of the game. But you remember the Litvinenko affair! Berezovsky was clearly the one being targeted. When it comes to revenge, Putin bides his time. Anyway, it gave you an excuse to come to London."

After what proved to be a delicious meal, Gwyneth retrieved her Bentley. In the car, she turned to Malko and said:

"Last time you were here, you took me to that unusual club on Brook Street, remember? Want to go again?"

It was an expensive discothèque, and somewhat special. A club where you could do whatever you pleased, provided you behaved appropriately. The last time, Gwyneth chose not to indulge, but apparently she retained a pleasant memory of the place.

"We could drop by," said Malko, who was also feeling turned on.

Twenty minutes later they pulled up at a nameless, polished

black door on Brook Street. Malko rang, and a Pakistani in a turban opened the door. He silently studied them for a few moments, then stepped aside. They headed down the stairs to a dimly lit basement occupied by red chairs and sofas, a long bar with a few men, and some dark booths. Soft music played as couples drank and flirted.

"Let's sit at the bar," suggested Gwyneth. "That way, we can see everything that's going on."

Easing herself onto a tall stool, she crossed her legs high enough to reveal most of her thigh. This caught the eye of the man sitting next to her, who was rummaging between a sexy redhead's legs.

Gwyneth leaned close, put her hand on Malko's crotch, and felt his cock.

"This place is a real turn-on!" she said huskily. "I'm in the mood to fuck. Specifically, I'm in the mood to fuck you. Look at my tits."

Seeing her long nipples straining against the silk blouse, he very lightly brushed them with his hand, which made them even stiffer.

Next to them, the couple could no longer keep their hands off each other.

"Let's go find a quiet corner," Gwyneth whispered. "These bar stools aren't very comfortable."

Just then a tall brunette appeared, wearing a long silk evening dress cut down her back to a pair of truly beautiful buttocks.

"Welcome!" she said. "I think I'll take you into the red room. You'll be more comfortable. Here you might shock the onlookers."

Without waiting for an answer, she took Gwyneth's hand and helped her off the stool, in the process exposing her panties for a second. Malko trailed the two women, admiring the brunette's magnificent ass.

She put her mouth to Gwyneth's ear and said, loud enough for Malko to hear:

"In case your friend gets a little tired, you'll find some boys here who are hung like bulls and full of Viagra."

The room was long and narrow, and even darker than the bar, with sofas on either side and mattresses on the floor.

The callipygous brunette settled them onto a sofa. On the couch across the way, a man was energetically working his girlfriend over, her thighs spread wide. Shadows were moving in the darkness: naked men with stiff cocks.

Gwyneth seemed to be in a daze. The brunette reached under the tweed skirt, deftly pulled off Gwyneth's black panties and stuffed them into her purse. The gesture seemed to drive the young American wild. She yanked Malko's zipper down, reached into his fly, and started steadily jerking him off.

A few men with impressive pricks came over to them. They stood in a circle, admiring Gwyneth's long legs while slowly caressing themselves.

She appeared to be fascinated by the closest pair of cocks pointed at her face. She closed her eyes and lost all her remaining self-control.

Ignoring the watching men, she drew out Malko's stiff cock and took it in her mouth. Her tongue was so skillful, he groaned with pleasure.

Two of the men with erections stepped closer.

Facing them, Gwyneth abruptly got to her feet and hiked up her skirt. Then she lowered herself onto Malko's cock, taking him all the way inside her. Knowing her tastes, he started pinching her long nipples, which produced a series of delighted sighs.

The two men came closer still, and were now jerking off just inches from her face.

Suddenly Gwyneth pulled Malko out of her cunt, moved him to her ass, and, with a hoarse sigh, slowly lowered herself onto him again. Then she seized the enormous cocks while Malko grabbed her hips and furiously thrust into her, eventually coming with a yell. Gwyneth released the two cocks and slumped back against him.

A long, relaxed pause.

"I've come as much as I can," she finally murmured. "Let's go home."

CHAPTER

4

Rem Tolkachev carefully reread the report from the Lon-
don *rezidentura* that the SVR had just delivered. It had been drafted
by the agent he'd assigned to handle the fallout from the Berezovsky
affair. This was Boris Tavetnoy, a reliable apparatchik who had
spent his entire career first in the KGB and then the SVR.

Up to now, everything had gone smoothly. The hands-off attitude taken by the British agencies on orders from above had mini-
mized the incident. A run-of-the-mill suicide, committed for
reasons unknown. The popular press had no reason to get excited
about the death of yet another émigré with a dubious past. True,
some of Berezovsky's friends claimed he'd been killed, but nobody
paid them much attention, and his family maintained a dignified
silence.

Alexander Litvinenko's widow had angrily complained about
the British courts' refusal to release any information that might
implicate Russia in her husband's murder. But that was a purely
British decision, and it didn't directly point to the motherland.

In writing his report, however, Tavetnoy raised a thorny problem that had to be dealt with. The CIA was apparently sticking its
nose into the Berezovsky affair, even though it wasn't involved.

Tolkachev had discovered the CIA's sniffing around thanks to
his habitual caution. To be on the safe side, the old spymaster had

ordered that everybody close to the late oligarch be put under surveillance by a special team of agents from Moscow, working with the London *rezidentura*.

Some of those people knew part of the truth, others had been directly or indirectly involved, and one in particular had some truly damning information. Until the affair completely died down, Tolkachev would have to proceed cautiously. He had no desire to stir up the controversy surrounding Litvinenko's death, for which Russia had been clearly responsible.

Fortunately, England now had a prime minister who was more pragmatic than his predecessor. David Cameron would apparently rather deal with Russia than confront it.

But the report from London summoned an old ghost that had already given Russia a lot of headaches: Malko Linge, the CIA operative who had investigated the Litvinenko case and discovered the truth about the former FSB agent's death.

As he did with all the people around Berezovsky, Tavetnoy was tapping the phone of Nikolai Glushkov, the late oligarch's best friend. So he learned that Linge had called asking to meet him, and that the Russian had agreed. Glushkov probably didn't know anything special about his friend's death, but he might know something else that would require the FSB to take countermeasures.

This was an urgent problem and had to be solved.

Under the circumstances, killing Glushkov was out of the question. A murder coming so soon after the Berezovsky "suicide" was bound to raise suspicions in the media, even if MI5 kept hands off.

Which left Linge. The Austrian operative knew the Litvinenko and Berezovsky files, so it made sense for the CIA to bring him in.

Tolkachev took Linge's dossier from his armored file cabinet and slowly leafed through it. The Agency mission leader had long stuck in Russia's craw while escaping several assassination attempts. Tolkachev saw that he might now have an unhoped-for opportunity to rid the *rodina* of an enemy, and do it in a foreign country, which would avoid Russia being immediately suspect. He closed the file and lit one of his pastel Sobranie cigarettes. He needed to think.

This was a decision he couldn't make on his own.

By the time he had smoked three Sobranies, he had put together an operation that could be launched very quickly. He took a sheet of paper, wrote a few lines in his small, neat handwriting, and rang for an orderly. When a man in black promptly appeared, Tolkachev handed him the envelope and said:

"Take this to the president's private secretary."

Only Vladimir Vladimirovich could make this decision, thought Tolkachev, and he hoped he would. The CIA operative had already caused Russia a great deal of harm, so killing him fell squarely within the purview of the president's new directive.

Taking advantage of one of London's rare sunny days, Malko walked from the Lanesborough and entered the Hilton's revolving doors at ten minutes to six. He hoped Glushkov would show up. Malko had a laundry list of questions to ask him, and especially wanted to know the whereabouts of Uri Dan.

As Malko entered the lobby, he nearly collided with a burly man in a raincoat and a dark hat who was coming the other way.

Stepping back with an apologetic smile, the man touched Malko's left arm as he passed. Malko felt a slight sting, like a pin-prick, but his mind was on his meeting with Glushkov and he didn't pay it any attention.

He stopped and glanced into the bar to the right of the entrance. There was nobody there, but he was early.

Walking toward the bar, Malko suddenly had a sensation of inner heat, as if his blood had suddenly warmed up. It wasn't unpleasant, but it felt bizarre. He stopped, trying to make sense of the strange feeling.

Suddenly he felt extremely weary, and his legs began to fail. As he staggered toward one of the bar's armchairs, his vision blurred and he started seeing double. The hotel's walls seemed to be buckling, the chandeliers swaying.

He was frozen in place, unable to take a step.

Then all sensation stopped and Malko tumbled into blackness.

Tolkachev unfolded the freshly deciphered message from the London *rezidentura* and read the printed one-line message with pleasure:

The subject has been dealt with.

He smoothed the sheet and fetched the Linge file. He clipped the message to the top sheet, closed the file, and returned it to his cabinet.

He then drafted a short note to a doctor working in the special FSB unit that had replaced the KGB's Thirteenth Department, which specialized in the development of poisons.

When Malko opened his eyes, at first all he could make out was a vague shape in the darkened room.

"Feeling better, Malko?"

The voice sounded familiar, but it took him a few seconds to realize that it belonged to Stanley Dexter, the London CIA station chief.

He tried to say, "Hello, Stanley," but produced only a series of disjointed grunts. That was when he realized how weak he was. He felt as if he were floating inside his skin.

As Malko's vision gradually cleared, he saw what looked like the white walls of a hospital room. An IV was hooked to his right arm, and his hand looked shrunken.

With an effort, he could again see himself in the Hilton lobby, suddenly feeling faint and collapsing. Dexter came closer, and Malko could now make out his face. He tried to smile, but his lips wouldn't obey him.

"Where am I?" he eventually managed to mumble.

"At University College Hospital," said Dexter. "In the intensive care unit. You very nearly died."

"Why?"

"Apparently you were poisoned. Given an injection. Do you remember anything like that?"

Malko racked his brains, trying to reconstruct the scene.

"I was entering the Hilton when a man with very dark eyes bumped into me. Then I felt a sting. But I saw the man's face. He wasn't trying to hide."

Dexter smiled gravely.

"He was obviously sure you were going to die. In fact, what happened was a miracle. When you collapsed, the hotel immediately called the paramedics. I happened to be phoning you just as they arrived, and one of the EMTs had the presence of mind to answer your phone and tell me what was happening.

"I understood right away, and told them to bring you here. It's one of the best hospitals in London."

"I know. I came here to see Alexander Litvinenko seven years ago."

Said Dexter:

"You're in the same department he was brought to. As soon as I was notified, I called the head of the department and told him it might be a criminal case.

"When you got to the hospital, they undressed you and carefully examined your entire body. They found a tiny puncture mark on your left arm, barely a millimeter wide, with fresh blood. An X-ray revealed a foreign body under the skin, and it was immediately excised. It turned out to be a tiny capsule made of an alloy of iridium and platinum, two metals that the human body doesn't reject.

"It was taken out and examined. It contained a liquid that would enter your body through two orifices too small to be seen with the naked eye."

"What was in the capsule?" asked Malko.

"Ricin. It's a powerful poison that would have entered your bloodstream. You would have died in a few days, in agony. If you'd been taken to another hospital, nobody would've thought to examine the pinprick."

"What happened then?"

"You've been given cortisone along with some other drugs, and a number of transfusions. You're out of danger now. You'll have to stay here for a few more days. After that, you can go back to the Lanesborough, assuming you want to stay on in London."

"Why would I leave?" asked Malko.

"Because I can't count on the Brits to protect you," said Dexter with a bitter smile. "I'm going to give you some bodyguards, of course, but it's not the same thing."

"Does MI5 know I was attacked?"

"I haven't told them anything, though they might learn it from other sources. Because of medical confidentiality, I don't think anyone here will talk."

Malko felt a little nauseated just then and had to close his eyes.

"I'm making you tired," said Dexter immediately. "I better go."

"No, no, it's nothing. I just feel very weak."

"Well, you barely pulled through. But it's an ill wind that blows no good."

"What do you mean?"

Dexter smiled coldly.

"Now we're positive that Boris Berezovsky didn't commit suicide, and there's more to learn about his death. Otherwise they wouldn't have tried to kill you."

"That's true."

A long silence followed, eventually broken by the station chief.

"Who knew that you were on your way to meet Glushkov?"

"No one. I phoned him, and nobody else knew besides you."

"Which means his line is bugged," said Dexter. "Also, that the Russians have an operational assassination team in London. Two days wouldn't have been enough for them to send a team from Moscow. So anybody who questions the Berezovsky suicide story is in danger. We'll have to take that into account.

"Could you recognize the man who tried to kill you?"

Malko closed his eyes and could visualize a man with a dark complexion and very dark eyes.

"Sure," he said. "He was about fifty, stocky, with a puffy face, full lips, a big nose, and piercing eyes."

Dexter nodded.

"When you're discharged, I'll show you the photos we have on file. We'll start with the members of the *rezidentura*, though I doubt they're involved; too risky. He's almost certainly a sleeper agent who has been here for a long time, maybe someone involved in the Berezovsky killing. It nearly cost you your life, but you moved the investigation a big step ahead.

"I'll leave you now. I'll come back tomorrow."

Dexter paused, then added:

"Oh, and I brought you something."

He took out a Beretta 92 in a GK holster and handed it to Malko.

"Put this under your pillow!" he said. "In any case, we'll have officers watching around the clock. I just hope the medical staff doesn't mention it to MI5."

Malko took the semiautomatic and slipped it under the sheets, though he felt too weak to use it.

Once he was alone, he checked his phone messages. Three of them were from Gwyneth Robertson, so he called and left a message on her voice mail. The former CIA case officer phoned back an hour later.

"Hi there," she said. "I was in a meeting. What's up? First you fuck me, then you forget me!"

"Somebody tried to kill me," said Malko. "I'm at University College Hospital."

He could hear her gasp.

"Did you get shot?" she asked anxiously.

"No, they tried to poison me. I'm not doing that well, but if you want to visit, I'm in Room 1312. But nobody can know I'm here."

"I'll see if I can come tomorrow," said Gwyneth. "Can I bring you anything?"

"Just yourself, but I'm not really feeling up to snuff."

Gwyneth gave a husky laugh, the kind that sparked orgasms.

"Don't worry, I won't try to jump your bones."

Tolkachev was so annoyed, he canceled his evening at the Bolshoi. The London *rezidentura* had combed the English press without finding any mention of Linge's death. Yet an agent at the scene saw him collapse in the Hilton lobby and watched as the EMTs arrived. Something had gone wrong, but what?

This Malko Linge person is a kind of curse, thought Tolkachev. But his anger at having failed gave way to a far more serious concern. Because Linge had survived, the CIA now knew Berezovsky hadn't committed suicide and would try harder than ever to expose the Russian operation. The British wouldn't get involved, but it would be very awkward if the CIA discovered the truth.

There was still some compromising evidence in London, Tolkachev knew. He had counted on things quieting down in a few weeks. Instead, he now found himself fighting a shadowy duel in which Russia's reputation was again at risk.

Though it made him sick, he drafted a note to the president explaining that there had been yet another slipup. Vladimir Putin would have to watch his step with London, while remaining cordial. The British might collaborate to a certain degree, but you couldn't wave a red flag at them.

And the spymaster still faced the problem of Malko Linge, who would now be on his guard. Would the operative continue his investigation? If so, Tolkachev would have to eliminate him, regardless of the risk.

CHAPTER

5

Malko was feeling very weak. The first time he tried to stand, he almost keeled over. There were red blotches on his face, and his left arm was swollen. He was still taking drugs to flush the ricin from his system.

Stanley Dexter gave him a worried look.

"Are you okay, Malko? Do you feel well enough to work?"

Two case officers had picked him up at University College Hospital and driven him first to the Lanesborough for a change of clothes, then to Grosvenor Square and the CIA offices.

"I'm ready," he said.

"In that case, follow me."

They went into a conference room where some thirty photos were spread out on a big table.

"These are the *rezidentura* people," said Dexter. "MI5 gave us the pictures, and they're up to date. Do you see your guy anywhere?"

Malko spent about ten minutes carefully studying the photographs, then announced:

"It's not any of these people. I'm sure of it."

"Okay, let's move on to the illegals. The Brits probably don't know about all of them, of course."

This time the pictures were in a bound album, and each page

had several photographs. Most were men, but there were a few women. Slowly turning the pages, Malko had almost reached the end when he stopped at a close-up of a man with a shaved head, a fleshy face, and heavy black eyebrows. He looked vaguely Asian.

"That's the man," he said. "I'm positive. Only he was wearing a hat, so I couldn't tell he was bald."

Dexter slid the photo out of its sleeve and read the few lines of information on the back.

"Arkady Lianin. First Directorate agent from 1986 to 1990. Was an agent in London for several years. Speaks perfect English, with a Cockney accent, even. Returned to Moscow and left the KGB in 1992 like many agents. At that point he disappeared. The British once spotted his photograph on a Moldovan passport in a phony name. He was coming from Brussels."

"Is he in London?" asked Malko.

Dexter smiled slightly.

"He must be, since he tried to kill you last week. When he asked England for political asylum, he claimed to have given up all intelligence activity. Worked for some private security companies for a few years. Then disappeared around 2004, officially leaving Great Britain.

"Nobody knows where he went. But in 2006, MI5 saw his picture on the Moldovan passport, which was used only once."

"So he's probably still working for the FSB," suggested Malko.

"That seems pretty clear, considering what happened to you. Problem is, we don't know where he is or what name or identity he's using. Lianin speaks English so well, it's easy for him to blend in."

"A man like that could very well have organized Berezovsky's assassination," said Malko.

"Sure, especially since he probably set up a network of other clandestine agents. But you now have an advantage: you can recognize him. The trick will be to find him."

A hush descended on the men. London had millions of inhabitants, and Arkady Lianin wasn't likely to approach Malko again.

"So what's your next move?" asked Dexter.

"Make another appointment with Glushkov," said Malko. "And try to contact Uri Dan, the bodyguard. After that, we'll see."

Said Dexter:

"I'm still waiting for the Riga station to send me information about the Latvian who's the boyfriend of Berezovsky's mistress. Maybe they'll turn something up."

Malko was already dialing Glushkov's number.

The Russian sounded surprised to hear from him.

"You stood me up!" he said. "Why didn't you come to the Hilton?"

"I apologize. I had a serious medical emergency and was out of commission for a couple of days. Can we make another date?"

Glushkov didn't need to be asked twice.

"How about tonight? Same time, same place?"

Rem Tolkachev was now receiving daily reports from London. The *rezidentura* had Linge under round-the-clock surveillance but hadn't been able to tap his cell phone. Things seemed to be settling down. There hadn't been any coverage of the attempted killing at the Hilton, and the Berezovsky affair was again fading into the background.

Nor had Vladimir Putin said anything about this new failure, which fortunately hadn't affected Russia's image.

But now Tolkachev faced a new dilemma. Thanks to the wiretaps, he knew that Glushkov had scheduled a new meeting with

Linge. So he had two options: allow the meeting to go ahead, or kill Glushkov first, which risked reviving the Berezovsky affair.

Tolkachev didn't see anything damaging in Glushkov's file that he might tell Linge, so he decided to stand pat—while hoping for the best.

Nor was the time right for attacking Linge again. He no longer traveled alone, Tolkachev knew. The CIA was guarding him, so he couldn't be touched for the time being.

Tolkachev decided to try a different approach, which involved Linge's room at the Lanesborough. There wouldn't be any direct contact this time, and if the plan worked, he would be rid of his CIA nemesis for good.

Malko immediately spotted Glushkov sitting in an armchair at the end of the bar. He was the only customer there. A small, stooped old man with a lined face, he didn't appear to be in good health. When Malko approached, he quickly stood up and shot him an inquisitive look.

"Are you the person who phoned me?" he asked in Russian.

"Yes, that was me. I was sick for a couple of days."

"The missed appointment isn't a problem," said Glushkov. "For a while I thought it was another of the tricks they pull to keep me off balance."

"Who do you mean, 'they'?"

Glushkov shot him a dark look.

"The people who killed Boris, those FSB bastards. When I was still in Moscow, they tried to kill me too, because I stuck by him."

"Did you two know each other well?"

"Yes, very well. We first met back in 1989, and we did business together. It was a time when you could make a lot of money."

Glushkov didn't mention spending three and a half years in jail for fraud and embezzlement.

"What did you do after that?" Malko asked.

"Business. I looked after some of Boris's affairs. We were very close. I'm the godfather of one of his daughters, Arina. He was like a brother to me."

"Do you have any thoughts about his death?"

Glushkov didn't hesitate for a second.

"It wasn't natural. He was killed on Putin's orders."

"Why?"

"For two reasons," said the Russian, lowering his voice. "First, because Putin has wanted to kill him for the last ten years. Second, because in a few weeks Boris was due to testify in the Litvinenko case, which is still open. He was going to reveal some important information that would have embarrassed Putin. That's reason enough, don't you think?"

"How do you suppose the killers did it?"

"I don't know," said Glushkov, "but I'm sure he was poisoned. That's the Russian way. They have all sorts of poisons. Some work fast, some slow, and they can't be detected—not like polonium. Inside Russia, the FSB does whatever it likes, because there's never an autopsy. I'm looking into that right now, with the help of some friends in Moscow."

"What do you think of the attitude of the British?"

"Those sons of bitches!" Glushkov exclaimed with a grimace of contempt. "Cameron gave Putin everything he wanted, ordering the police to hush things up. Nothing will come out from that side."

After a brief silence, Malko remarked:

"There is one person who knows more about Mr. Berezovsky's death than anybody: the man who found his body."

Glushkov's face darkened.

"Uri Dan, of course."

"Didn't he tell you anything?"

"He said the British police forbade him from telling anyone what he saw."

"Not even you?"

The Russian nodded.

"Uri and I weren't close. He knew I was Boris's best friend, of course, but that's all."

That struck Malko as odd.

"Do you know where I can find him?" he asked.

"I think he left London. I couldn't make it to Boris's funeral a few days ago, so I called Uri, who was there. He described the ceremony for me. He also said he was leaving England and going back to Israel."

"Do you have his cell number?"

"Yes, I often called him when I wasn't able to reach Boris. I knew that Uri was always with him."

"Did Mr. Berezovsky trust him?"

Glushkov seemed surprised by the question.

"I think so, yes," he said after a moment's thought. "Uri worked for him for several years. Boris often traveled to Israel. He spoke Hebrew and had many contacts there. He was Jewish, as you know."

"Can you give me Dan's phone number?"

Glushkov gave it to him.

It was the start of the beginning of a lead.

Glushkov was looking at him curiously.

"Who are you working for, anyway?" he asked.

"The Central Intelligence Agency."

"Why are they interested in Boris's death? He didn't have any connection with the CIA."

"Actually, the Agency is more interested in Russian activities abroad. The Americans feel that the Cold War is heating up again, and they're bothered that there might be clandestine FSB cells in Great Britain. I handled the Litvinenko affair, so they gave me the assignment."

"Good luck to you, then!" said Glushkov. "If I can be of any help, it'll be a pleasure. And now I have to leave you; I'm off to see *A Chorus Line* at the theater. Call me anytime you like."

The two men exchanged a warm handshake, and the old Russian headed for the exit, now walking very erect.

When he was alone, Malko dialed Dan's cell phone. A recorded female voice informed him that the number was not in service.

A great start, he thought gloomily.

Malko left the Hilton and caught a cab from the stand in front of the Dorchester, headed for the American embassy.

"I'll immediately alert our Tel Aviv station," said Dexter. "If we can get hold of Dan, we'll be way ahead of the game. If he traveled under his own name, we have a chance of finding him."

"Will the Israelis cooperate?" asked Malko.

The station chief looked dubious.

"I'm not sure it's a good idea to tell them. Jews tend to stick together."

"There is one other possibility," suggested Malko. "Michael Cherney, Berezovsky's friend. Cherney made the hotel reservation for him. Maybe he knows the bodyguard."

"I'll ask the station to put somebody on it," said Dexter. "And you're right, Cherney might be inclined to work with us. After all, he was Berezovsky's friend."

"Meanwhile, I don't have anything else to do," said Malko. "The family is lying low, and I don't have a contact for his girlfriend, even assuming she has anything to do with this."

"I might have something on her," said the station chief. "I'll ask my secretary."

A few moments later, she brought them the Berezovsky file. Dexter took out a page and handed it to Malko.

"Here you go. Anita Spiridanova is being represented by a local public relations agency. They're handling her professional profile. You could pretend to be a reporter and try to meet her. I hear she's very pretty."

"That's not quite reason enough, but I'll give it a try."

Malko wrote down the phone number and left Dexter's office. He didn't bother mentioning that he was having dinner with Gwyneth Robertson.

CHAPTER

6

"You've lost weight!" exclaimed Gwyneth. "I'm taking you to the Connaught. They serve the best roast beef in London. The mood's a bit fusty, but the meat's incredible."

When Malko got into the Bentley, he saw that Gwyneth was wearing office attire: an ankle-length gray dress, boots—the weather in London was still awful—and a minimum of makeup. But she had that incredible fuck-me look of a she-cat in heat.

At the Connaught, she handed the Bentley key to a polite, blasé valet and headed for the old hotel's dining room, which was low-key and full of businesspeople. A waiter wheeled a cart to their table and gravely rolled the lid from a chafing dish, revealing a magnificent slab of beef.

When he left, Gwyneth said:

"I had dinner with one of my old MI5 pals last night, James Stillwell. I got to know him during the Litvinenko case."

"A friend or a lover?" asked Malko with a slight smile.

"He's very charming," she admitted. "We had a little thing back in the day. He was crazy about me, but it wasn't quite mutual. He's decided to try warming it up again."

"This is your private life, Gwyn. Why are you telling me about it?"

"Because it's not entirely private," she said. "I didn't accept

James's invitation on a whim. He's been with the MI5 section that handles Russian émigrés in Britain for a few years, and he now heads the department. I thought it might be useful for you."

"It certainly would!" Malko exclaimed. "But did he tell you anything?"

"A man in love always lets his guard down a little," Gwyneth said with a smile. "As you might imagine, I steered the conversation around to Berezovsky's death."

Malko had lost all interest in his roast beef.

"What did he say?"

"Pretty much what we suspected, that MI5 got orders from Downing Street not to push things. The prime minister's deal is, the Russians will cooperate on terrorism if the English turn a blind eye to their little escapades."

"Killing a man is hardly an escapade."

Gwyneth took a big bite of her roast beef.

"In the eyes of the British it is," she said quite seriously. "Unlike the Litvinenko affair, there wasn't any scandal with Berezovsky. It was just an ordinary suicide, by a guy with a lousy reputation. Even the family didn't make a stink. The only people who called it murder were Berezovsky's pals, and they'd been involved in shady deals themselves. The tabloids didn't get excited. So MI5 has it all wrapped up."

"Did Stillwell tell you what Berezovsky died of?"

The young American shook her head.

"No. He says the file is still in the hands of the local police."

"What about toxicology results?"

"They sent the samples to a government laboratory, so it might take months to get test results, maybe years—if ever. Landing the Sochi Olympics security gig was worth some sacrifices, apparently. The only person who thought Berezovsky was a wonderful person was Lisa, one of his daughters."

"So your dinner date didn't turn up much."

"No, except that we're now positive about the Brits' attitude."

"Did you tell Stillwell what happened to me at the Hilton?"

Gwyneth shook her head.

"No, I didn't. I didn't even mention you. He wouldn't have liked hearing that. My hunch is, MI5 doesn't know. In any case, you can't expect anything from them."

"That I already knew," said a disappointed Malko.

Then he suddenly remembered something that would greatly help the investigation.

"Gwyneth, there's something I didn't tell you," he said. "I've identified the man who tried to poison me."

"Really? How did you do that?"

"Actually, the Agency did. MI5 gave them pictures of the sleeper Russian agents in London, and Dexter showed them to me. His name is Arkady Lianin. A former KGB agent, now with the FSB."

Malko summarized what little was known about the agent and concluded:

"We would love to get hold of him. I'm almost positive he's involved in the Berezovsky affair."

Gwyneth wrote the name in her notebook, then glanced up, grinning.

"I bet James knows the guy, though he might not know where he is. I'll see if I can worm it out of him. Only it's going to cost me. I'll have to be very sweet to him."

She looked Malko in the eye, making it clear that he was pushing her into another man's arms.

"I'm sure you can promise without delivering," he said evasively.

Gwyneth didn't comment. Instead she said, almost to herself:

"The only way I'll find out anything about this Lianin character will be if I tell James it's a request by the Agency and completely unconnected to the Berezovsky affair. Or to you."

"Please do whatever you can," said Malko.

Having finished their roast beef, they had strawberries and cream for dessert, and Malko asked for the check.

It was huge.

London was living up to its reputation as the most expensive city in the world.

Gwyneth drove down South Audley Street to Piccadilly, then turned right toward Hyde Park Corner. But instead of stopping in front of the Lanesborough, she continued west on Knightsbridge Road.

At Malko's puzzled look, she smiled and said:

"I want to show you my new place. It's in Chelsea."

Gwyneth might like James Stillwell, but she clearly wasn't in love with him.

It was late, but there were still quite a few people at the Lanesborough's Library Bar. In the front room, two men were sitting on stools, drinking tomato juice and ogling a trio of gorgeous hookers who had come in from the cold and were sipping sodas.

One of the men answered his phone, listened for a moment, and promptly asked for the check. Moments later, the two left the bar and headed for the elevator.

They got off at the fourth floor. The landing was empty, except for a man sitting in an armchair, who stood up and joined them. The trio walked down the left-hand hallway and stopped in front of Room 418.

The third man took a rectangular box from his bag and pressed it against the door lock. It hummed softly for a moment, then flashed a green ready light. He took a magnetic key from his pocket and put it in the slot. The bolt slid back with a click, and the door to Room 418 was open.

His task done, the man who had picked the lock with the electronic passkey put his gear away and left. One of the other two went to stand guard at the end of the hall, near the elevator, while his partner went into the room.

Once inside, he got to work with no fear of being surprised. A second team was watching Malko Linge, and had passed the word that the CIA man and his dinner date were in a house in Chelsea.

From his briefcase, the man took a pair of double-lined rubber gloves and carefully slipped them on. Then he put on a kind of gas mask, a sophisticated respirator dosed with a powerful antidote.

He was playing with his life.

He took a glass capsule containing about a milligram of a deadly organophosphate nerve agent. Similar to sarin, it was made under FSB supervision at a military chemistry plant in the closed city of Shikhany in the Saratov region. When diffused in the air, it blocked the victim's nervous impulses, first contracting the pupils, then paralyzing the nervous system. A postmortem examination would conclude the death was caused by a cerebral embolism.

Without lifting the room telephone handset, the man opened the capsule and let a tiny drop of the liquid fall onto the plastic mouthpiece. Then he carefully closed the capsule and stowed it in his briefcase, followed by the gas mask and rubber gloves. His work was done.

When the phone was used next, heat from the person's face or mouth would activate the poison.

The man closed his briefcase, switched off the lights, and joined his partner in the hall. They took the elevator downstairs, crossed the lobby, and walked off down Knightsbridge Road.

All they had to do now was dial the room number. When Malko answered, he would inhale the poison and die within seconds.

———

Gwyneth set a breakfast tray with a teapot and toast on her bed.

"You can ride with me into town if you like," she said. "I make a good living, but I start early. Otherwise, you can sleep late and take a taxi."

Malko looked at his watch: it was seven thirty. The night before, they had reached Gwyneth's place around eleven, but didn't go to sleep until much later.

It was a charming little town house in Chelsea, and—miracle of miracles—even had a parking space in front for the Bentley. This being London, no one scratched or vandalized the car, nor would they dream of taking Gwyneth's parking place.

"I'll ride in with you," said Malko, stretching.

Twenty minutes later, they were heading to central London in heavy traffic. Despite the congestion charge—a stiff tax on vehicles entering central London—a lot of people were on the road.

"I'm going to call James today," promised Gwyneth. "I'm sure he'll be delighted to have lunch with me, or, rather, dinner. Only I won't be able to raise the subject of your Arkady Lianin right away. It might take several days. But I'm sure James has a file on him."

"That would be a stroke of luck," said Malko. "MI5 swore up and down to the CIA that they had lost him and he might not even be in England."

"Well, we know he is," she said. "You can count on me."

A good half hour later, the Bentley stopped in front of the Lanesborough. Gwyneth kissed Malko on the lips, with a sly smile.

"Don't bother asking me to dinner for a few days; I'll be busy."

Just the same, he stroked her thigh before getting out of the car.

Despite Gwyneth's promises, his investigation was on hold. Going up to his room, he found the *Times* hanging on his door-knob and headed directly for the bathroom. So as not to make

Gwyneth late, he hadn't bothered to shower or shave at her place. Under the hot water, he thought back to the man who had tried to poison him, increasingly convinced that he was involved in Berezovsky's "suicide."

A text appeared on Malko's cell phone:

Come to Grosvenor Square. Stanley.

It was nearly eleven a.m. The CIA station chief hadn't phoned, so he must have important news. Within minutes, Malko was in a taxi.

Dexter greeted him with a satisfied smile.

"We tracked down the bodyguard," he said.

CHAPTER

7

Stanley Dexter waved Malko over to the big leather sofa next to the coffee table, then sat down himself.

"Is Dan still in London?" asked Malko.

"No, but by tracking his plane ticket, we know where he went. He left London the day after Berezovsky's funeral. MI5 helped arrange his departure from Heathrow. He took a direct El Al flight to Tel Aviv."

"And after that?"

"We knew Dan used to work for the Mossad, so the Tel Aviv station asked for their help. It was easy for them. He'd kept a little apartment in Tel Aviv, and they gave us the address."

"What about a phone number?"

"No dice. They wouldn't take cooperation that far," said Dexter. "And they made us promise not to mention it."

"Does Dan know we're interested in him?"

"Not unless the Mossad tipped him off."

"So what do you suggest?"

"The weather's a lot nicer in Tel Aviv than here," said the CIA station chief with a smile. "I think it would be an excellent idea for you to go ask him some questions. The local station can provide support."

"And you're sure there's nothing else for me to do here in London?"

"There probably is, but talking to Dan is a priority. He might disappear from one moment to the next. It would be best if you left tomorrow."

The station chief was making more than a suggestion, Malko realized. Aside from the police, the Israeli bodyguard was the only person to have seen Boris Berezovsky's body, and therefore the only person to describe it in detail. Malko thought of Gwyneth. He absolutely had to see her before he left to find out if she'd learned anything about Arkady Lianin. That trail could also greatly advance his investigation.

"Very well," he said. "I'll catch an early flight to Tel Aviv tomorrow."

Malko was getting to his feet when Dexter stopped him.

"Hold on a minute, Malko. Before you go, I'd like you to talk to an NCS man who made a special trip to London for this case. His name's Ryan Young."

"What is he here for?" asked Malko, wondering why the National Clandestine Service would be called in.

"He specializes in dirty tricks and black bag jobs," said Dexter. "He's done quite a few for the Agency. We asked him to study the Berezovsky suicide, assume it was actually a murder in disguise, and tell us how he would've done it. Are you okay with seeing him?"

"Of course!"

The station chief stepped out and returned with a heavyset man with black hair, chubby cheeks, and slightly prominent blue eyes. The NCS specialist looked like a retired factory foreman.

Dexter made the introductions.

"Ryan here is a very sneaky guy," he said. "He may be able to enlighten us."

Young asked Malko where he wanted him to start.

"With the bathroom," he said. "I'm going to interview the bodyguard, so I'm interested in your thoughts about the death scene."

Young opened a folder where he had noted some points of interest.

"I haven't been on site, so I don't have any details beyond what the police released," he began. "But I've considered a number of things. First, the fact that the bathroom door was locked from the inside suggests that Berezovsky locked himself in. That actually doesn't mean squat one way or the other. We have B and E guys who pick locks using special tools that only leave microscopic scratches. I assume the Russians have people who are as good as ours. So the door could easily have been locked from outside the bathroom."

"What about the hanging itself?" asked Malko.

Young made a face.

"Two main things about it struck me as strange," he said. "When you hang yourself, you usually stand on something, but there's been no mention of a chair or a stool. Also, to hang himself, the shower pipe and the cord had to be strong enough to support Berezovsky's weight. Then there's this: the police reported that he was found lying on the floor with a broken rib. The rib supposedly broke when he fell, and he fell because the rope broke. That scenario doesn't make any sense. If the rope broke, it's more than likely that Berezovsky was still alive when he hit the floor. Breaking a rib hurts like hell. So why didn't he react to the pain, if he was still alive? The only explanation is that he was already dead when he fell or was thrown to the floor. He didn't die of strangulation, but from something else. If we assume this was murder, I'd bet it was poison."

The age-old Russian method, thought Malko. Poisonings had

been used to settle scores in Russia and the Soviet Union for ages, with Alexander Litvinenko just one of the most recent victims.

"Tell me something, Ryan," Malko said. "If you'd been asked to do this job, would you take it on?

"Sure, no problem," said Young promptly. "All you need is careful preparation and a good team. Especially since the bodyguard was away for several hours, leaving his boss alone at the estate."

"What about the security cameras?"

Young snorted with laughter.

"I've spent my life neutralizing cameras and alarm systems," he said. "For a while, my job was breaking into foreign embassies in Washington. There were plenty of cameras and alarms, and they never gave us any problems."

Very edifying, thought Malko.

"So speaking as a professional, you think it's likely that Berezovsky was murdered?"

"Affirmative."

"Thanks very much for your time, Ryan," said Malko. "I appreciate your coming to London."

But the NCS specialist stopped him.

"Just one more thing, sir. I went through the case file pretty carefully, and there's something I'd like to mention. It might help your investigation."

"What's that?"

From his briefcase, Young took a file containing newspaper clippings, some of them highlighted in yellow.

"We know that on the evening before his death, Berezovsky saw a journalist from *Forbes Russia*, Ilya Sokolov, who made a special trip from Moscow to interview him at the Four Seasons. People thought that odd, because *Forbes* wasn't on very good terms with Berezovsky. What did you make of it, sir?"

"I figured Sokolov was probably supporting the plot against

him," answered Malko. "Soon after Berezovsky's death, word spread that he was bankrupt and feeling discouraged and suicidal. That looks like Russian disinformation, to lend credence to the suicide thesis. Same thing with the letter he supposedly wrote to Putin, asking permission to come home because he was washed up. The Russians are old hands at that kind of stage setting."

"I'm sure you're right, sir," said Young, "especially since nobody knows what Berezovsky and Sokolov talked about.

"But something about that meeting intrigued me. So I had the Agency translate the *Forbes* article from Russian, and I read it very carefully. Guess what? There's nothing in the article that would justify asking for a last-minute interview. There were no revelations, aside from the comments on Mr. Berezovsky's state of mind, and they only became significant after he died. Yet Sokolov is considered a first-rate journalist in Russia. He doesn't waste his time publishing bullshit."

"So what do you conclude from this?" asked Malko.

"When you're preparing a wet job like this one, the first thing you've got to do is localize your target with absolute certainty."

"What do you mean?"

Young explained:

"The Russian kill team had to know for sure where Berezovsky would be spending that night. It could have been lots of places. He had two girlfriends in town, he had friends, he might stay at a hotel or go home, which is what he eventually did. But the elimination team had to be positive. Best way to do that would be to follow him when he left the Four Seasons and see where he went. For a well-trained team, it's a piece of cake. And it lets them strike with certainty."

Malko's mind was now racing.

"Are you saying that the only purpose of the interview was to take charge of Berezovsky, to determine where he would be in the coming hours?"

"If it were my gig, that's what I would've done," said Young.

"So Sokolov could have played a much more active role in this case than we suspected?"

"That's what I think."

The NCS man's suggestion made perfect sense, thought Malko, and it fit what he knew of the Russians' modus operandi. If someone had asked Sokolov to go to England to interview Berezovsky, he would certainly do it.

"Thanks very much for this," he said. "I'll take it into account in my investigation. Unfortunately, Sokolov has gone back to Russia and probably isn't easy to reach there."

"That's too bad," said Young. "But I hope I've been helpful. Good luck!"

After the NCS specialist left the office, Dexter said:

"I'm starting to think maybe you should go to Moscow!"

Malko smiled.

"I'm going to Tel Aviv first. If I show up in Moscow, the Russians will immediately suspect we're investigating Berezovsky's death."

"They know that already, and the attempt to poison you proves it," said Dexter. "But all right, we'll do things in order. Meanwhile, I'll ask the Moscow station what they can find out about Sokolov."

He went to his desk and rang his secretary.

"Mary, Mr. Linge is leaving. Do you have what he needs?"

Moments later the secretary brought an envelope and handed it to Malko, saying:

"This has your ticket for Tel Aviv, a reservation at the Dan Hotel, and a list of useful phone numbers."

Dexter said:

"Someone from the station will meet you at Ben Gurion. Enjoy the sunshine."

Leaving the embassy "bunker," Malko hailed a cab on Upper Grosvenor Street and called Gwyneth Robertson.

"I'm in a meeting," she said. "Any new developments?"

"I'm leaving London tomorrow morning. I'd like to see you this evening."

She thought for a few seconds, then said:

"All right, but it won't be before nine thirty. At the Caprice on Arlington Street near Piccadilly. Catch you later!"

The Caprice turned out to be a kind of British brasserie that was so noisy, it felt like being at a cattle auction. Everyone was shouting. An Asian maître d' informed Malko that Miss Robertson's table wasn't ready and parked him at the bar.

Gwyneth breezed in at ten to ten, loaded down with file folders. She plunked them on a bar stool next to Malko and sighed.

"If it weren't you, I would've gone straight home to bed! I'm beat."

To the bartender she said:

"A double vodka martini, please, and something to eat. I'm starving."

She was wearing her office combat uniform: a Chanel suit with a fuchsia-colored blouse stretched taut over her large breasts. She surreptitiously parted the blouse to give Malko a glimpse of her bra.

"See? It matches! The panties, too."

With Gwyneth, eroticism was always just below the surface.

A few moments later they were led to a small table in the back that had just been cleared.

She looked at Malko with a sarcastic grin.

"I know your desire to see me isn't completely disinterested, but I love you anyway. Where are you off to tomorrow?"

"Tel Aviv."

"The bodyguard?"

Gwyneth didn't miss a trick.

"That's right. The Agency tracked him down, but I don't know if he'll talk to me. What's happening at your end?"

She sipped her martini and smiled.

"I'm sacrificing what little virtue I have left to try to locate Arkady Lianin."

"Are you getting anywhere?"

She scowled at him playfully.

"You want a play-by-play on exactly how James is doing? Now that he's gotten to home plate, he's gone crazy. Won't leave me alone. I hope he doesn't talk about this at work. People might start to wonder."

"Have you gotten anything from him?" Malko asked cautiously.

"For the time being, he's the one who's getting something from me. We're in the approach phase. The sting will come later, maybe when you come back, if you stay long enough."

"I'm really sorry for what I'm putting you through," said Malko.

"Don't sweat it. He's a very good lover, so it isn't exactly a chore. I saw a gorgeous brooch in a magazine, and he rushed off to Harrods to buy it for me. He's spending his retirement savings."

Though the former CIA case officer was being pleasantly cynical, she did wonder if she was hurting Malko's feelings. Putting her hand on his, she said, almost tenderly:

"I'll still enjoy making love with you when you come back. James is just on probation. If he has the necessary information, we'll locate Lianin."

A waiter brought them some curried shrimp and rice, and Gwyneth tore into it, eating like a truck driver. A clergyman to their right ogled her chest as he ate.

By the time Gwyneth reached her lemon meringue pie, she had relaxed a bit.

"I'm going to gently start raising the pressure on James," she said. "He's too much in love to bail out now. Provided he has the information, of course."

The restaurant was emptying. When they left, it was nearly midnight.

"I'll drop you off," she said.

A valet had already brought the Bentley, which smelled of her perfume. The moment he was seated, Malko couldn't help putting his hand on the young woman's thigh.

"Don't get any ideas," she said with a giggle. "I'm coming from the office, and I'm wearing pantyhose!"

Rem Tolkachev opened the envelope that had just come from the FSB on Bolshaya Lubyanka Street. The note from the London *rezidentura* informed him that Malko Linge had taken a flight for Tel Aviv two hours earlier.

He put the note down and started to think. He knew perfectly well why Linge was going to Israel, and he was furious.

What was the point of neutering the damned English if the CIA was going to come down on him? Especially with a man like Linge!

The spymaster now had to weigh the risks of possible counter-measures. Plus, he had suffered another reversal. The steps he had ordered be carried out to eliminate Linge in London apparently hadn't worked. He had to wind down that operation at any cost, or face another failure.

CHAPTER 8

"Housekeeping!"

With that warning shout, Benazir Saldo opened the door to Room 418. The chambermaid knew it was empty, since the guest had checked out that morning, but calling a warning was second nature to her. Hotel staff never entered a room without doing so, and the Lanesborough strictly enforced the rule.

Saldo propped the door open and began cleaning the suite, starting with the bathroom.

The young Pakistani woman had been working at the Lanesborough for six months, and she performed her tedious work with almost obsessive dedication. It was a job she wanted to keep.

Everything went as usual until she got to the hanging closet. When she opened it, she noticed what looked like currency sticking out of the safe. Reaching in, she picked up a small roll of ten-pound notes that the guest must have forgotten.

Though the bills represented half her weekly salary, Saldo was tempted only for a few seconds. First, because she was honest, and second, because the money could have been left there deliberately, to trap her.

Putting the notes back, she walked over to the night table, picked up the house phone, and pressed the "Housekeeping" button.

When her supervisor answered, she said, "This is Benazir Saldo. I am in Room 418, and I just found some money that was left in the room safe. Can you please send somebody to fetch it?"

"Certainly," he said. "I'll come up myself."

The young maid hung up and continued with her cleaning, carefully making the bed.

It wasn't until a few minutes later that she felt a strange vertigo. At first, she thought it was just a momentary dizziness and forced herself to go on working. But her legs began to fail and her head spun. Though it was against the rules, she dropped into an armchair, unable to move. Her face was covered with sweat, and she could feel her heart racing.

Hearing someone enter the room, Saldo tried to stand up, but a fresh wave of vertigo hit, and she collapsed onto the deep carpet. Her supervisor found her sprawled on the floor at the foot of the bed.

"My God!" he exclaimed.

From the chambermaid's pallor, he immediately realized that she was gravely ill. He pulled out his cell phone and called security directly.

"I'm in Room 418 with a sick employee, and it seems serious. Send a paramedic right away!"

Saldo was no longer moving. The supervisor took her pulse and found it very faint. Though still breathing, she was obviously in bad shape. While waiting for the paramedics, he retrieved the pound notes from the safe and put them in a hotel envelope marked with the room number.

A few minutes later, a nurse and an EMT came in with a stretcher for Saldo. After they left, the supervisor checked to see that the room had been made up, and left. He decided the chambermaid might just be pregnant, and thought no more about it.

———

Arriving on a British Airways flight from London, Malko entered the interminable circular hallway that served Ben Gurion Airport's arrival gates. Hordes of travelers were pouring in from the four corners of the world or milling about, looking for their departure gates. It felt like being in a subway.

He reached the arrivals area along with a heterogeneous crowd of tourists, black-clad Orthodox Jews, and businesspeople.

Malko felt slightly on edge. Despite their legendary caution, the last time he'd been in Israel, the Israelis had tried to kill him.

The lines at immigration were long, and Malko resigned himself to waiting. After half an hour, an impassive immigration officer took his passport, scanned it, asked Malko if he consented to its being stamped. Then he returned it.

Malko was traveling with only carry-on luggage, so he headed directly for the exit. In the crowd of people waiting for arriving passengers he saw a young man holding up a sign with his name.

"I'm John Harding, one of Oliver Snow's deputies," said the man, a young American. "He asked me to help you check into the Dan, then bring you to the embassy. He's expecting you for an early dinner."

A few minutes later they were on the freeway leading to Tel Aviv, in brilliant sunshine. The closer they got to the city, the worse the traffic.

"Getting into town is a nightmare," Harding said. "They were supposed to build a train between Jerusalem and Tel Aviv, but it never happened."

Malko looked at the arid landscape around him. A commuter rail line ran along the freeway. There were factories everywhere, a hive of activity.

"What's the mood in the country like?" he asked.

"Pretty bad," said Harding. "Most people are just scraping by. There's no money. Here in Tel Aviv, the Israelis don't think about the Arabs much. They never see any, except for Israeli Arabs, and the West Bank is far away. All the people here want to do is party and get rich."

They passed two hitchhiking soldiers in uniform, Galil assault rifles on their shoulders.

A common sight.

Exiting the freeway, Harding headed for downtown.

A blazing late-afternoon sun shone through the tinted windows of the American embassy, which stood above one of Tel Aviv's most popular beaches.

A series of terraces separated the embassy from Herbert Samuel Street, the beachside promenade, with its falafel stands, beachwear shops, and inexpensive restaurants. A different world.

The building was squeezed between the beach and narrow, noisy Hayarkon Street. Not only was the street always jammed, it was also one-way, which didn't make getting around any easier.

For some reason, the embassy had been built in the most touristy part of Tel Aviv, near the opera and a trio of luxury hotels: the Hilton, the Sheraton, and the Dan, where Malko was staying.

Though located in a friendly country, the embassy's security precautions were extreme, even though it had never been attacked. Hamas militants would be the only ones so inclined, and they hadn't yet reached Tel Aviv.

The building itself was fortified on all sides and protected by a swarm of electronic devices: a secure bubble in the middle of a hostile world. Its flat roof, which bristled with antennas, also served as a heliport. That made it a lot easier to infiltrate CIA operatives into Israel and discreetly fly out friendly Palestinians being pursued by Shin Bet. The embassy's location at the water's edge simplified many things.

The United States and Israel were allies, but each side kept a few secrets from the other.

When Malko entered the dining room, Oliver Snow was gazing at the Mediterranean through one of the large picture windows. The CIA station chief turned and came over, smiling warmly.

"Hello, Malko!" he said. "We met briefly about two years ago. I'll be here for another year before I head back to Langley."

The station chief was a lanky, somewhat austere-looking man with a long jaw and brown hair. He wore square rimless glasses and a pinstripe suit.

The two men sat down at the big dining table. A Marine waiter brought a bottle of Chablis.

"Welcome to Tel Aviv," said Snow, raising his glass. "I think your mission here will be pretty simple. But first, let's have something to eat. I know it's early, but I figured you might be hungry."

They served themselves from a long buffet table with grilled, fried, and steamed fish, a selection of Middle Eastern mezes, and American-style salads.

Attentive Marine waiters stood at either end of the table.

As the two men ate, they talked about the region's problems, including the stalled Israeli-Palestinian talks, which had been at a standstill for years because of Israeli intransigence.

"How did President Obama's visit go?" asked Malko.

The American president had made a lightning visit to Israel a few weeks earlier.

"It was a nonevent," said Snow with a sigh. "The president doesn't want to get enmeshed in a process he doesn't believe in. Nobody had any great expectations, neither the Israelis nor the Palestinians. Netanyahu doesn't like Obama and Obama doesn't like Netanyahu, and that's it."

"What about Syria?"

The CIA station chief sighed again.

"That's a different story! The Israelis basically get along with the Syrians. In thirty years of cold war, there's never been a major incident between the two countries. When you come right down to it, Israel would be just as happy if al-Assad stayed in power, even if they claim the contrary. Particularly since Assad's army has been quite successful on the ground. Everyone expected his regime to collapse very quickly, and a lot of countries are now having painful second thoughts. Nobody wants to see al-Qaeda set up shop in Syria, the Israelis least of all."

Snow continued:

"We were foolish to jump on board the anti-Assad bandwagon so fast. Now we're trying to put together that damn conference in Geneva, and it's not happening. Besides, it assumes that the problem will be solved, and that Assad is prepared to step down, which isn't the case at all.

"Millions of Arabs would like to wipe Israel off the face of the Middle East, but nobody has the military power to do it. Same thing with Assad. As long as the Russians and the Iranians back him, he can hang on indefinitely."

This wasn't exactly the official American position, thought Malko. The United States was calling daily for the Syrian president to resign.

"So the Israelis aren't too worried," he said aloud.

"No, especially since things inside Israel are pretty calm, and events are going their way. They're working day and night to colonize the West Bank while trying not to make it look obvious. They hope to make the situation there irreversible. Actually, it already is. Go take a look sometime. You'll see a patchwork of Palestinian villages and Israeli settlements, too entangled to pull apart."

"Don't the Palestinians protest?"

"They're resigned," said Snow. "Thanks to the truckloads of cash sent by the European Union, they're living a little better. The

Israelis have eliminated the most annoying checkpoints, and Ramallah, the so-called capital, is awash with money."

"What about Hamas?"

"They're as happy as clams at high tide," said the station chief. "They never did want to negotiate with Israel. And with Qatar coming in on their side, they're also getting money and weapons, so they're gathering their forces for a final confrontation. The borders with Egypt have opened a bit, and life is a little easier.

"I think Israel's only real fear is that Mahmoud Abbas will hand over the keys to the West Bank, which would force them to run the territory. That would be an economic nightmare, because the situation in Israel is already pretty grim. I know families who are living on three thousand shekels a month. There are pockets of poverty along the coast, and wages are very low."

Snow gestured to the waiter to pour them more wine, then said:

"Let's get back to the ranch. The London station says you're here to meet an Israeli named Uri Dan who was Boris Berezovsky's bodyguard."

"That's right," said Malko. "The Agency is interested in the affair, and I think the man who actually found Berezovsky's body might have things to tell me. If he's willing to talk, that is."

Snow said:

"When I got the message from London, I called one of my counterparts in the Mossad, because I knew Dan had worked for them for a few years. He was willing to give me his address but said Dan no longer had any connection with the Institute. Since leaving the Mossad, he's worked for a number of private security companies."

"Did they ask the reason for your request?"

"Yes, of course. I told them the truth. I said the Agency wanted to ask him some questions about Berezovsky's death. That didn't seem to be a problem for them."

This is too good to be true, thought Malko.

"So what's our next step?" he asked.

"We don't know if Dan has a new job, so you'll have to see him at home. My deputy John Harding will drive you; he knows the city very well. But I suggest you try one thing first. We have a source who follows the doings of all the ex-Mossad people, a *Haaretz* reporter named Yossi Milton. With any luck, he'll have some information on Dan. Milton knows John and will be waiting for you in front of the Habima Theatre at five o'clock.

"Until then, you can go lie on the beach."

Looking out at the blue sweep of the Mediterranean, with people playing in the waves, a person would never think he was in a country at war surrounded by hostile neighbors.

The mission was getting off to a pretty good start, thought Malko. The Israelis had no special reason to be interested in Berezovsky's death. They didn't have to provide the ex-Mossad man's address, but they had.

"I have to leave you now," said the CIA station chief. "John will pick you up at your hotel in an hour. Good luck!"

"So what do we do about the schmuck?" asked Dov Burg, the Tel Aviv Shin Bet chief.

"We watch and wait," answered Amir Peretz, Shin Bet's liaison officer with the Mossad. The Mossad wasn't authorized to operate within Israel, so when the CIA asked about Uri Dan, Peretz had passed the query on to Burg.

Initially, the request caused no particular concern. Dan had left the Mossad long before, didn't know any state secrets, and had been working in the private sector for some years, like many former Mossad agents.

But the Israelis sat up and took notice when they learned that Malko Linge was in the country. The CIA operative was on a list of people considered to be enemies of Israel and had been immediately flagged by immigration at Ben Gurion Airport. An enemy, but one to be handled carefully, since he worked for the CIA, a nominally friendly organization.

From the moment Malko left the airport, a Shin Bet team had followed him to the Dan Hotel and then to the American embassy. There the trail went cold, as the Israelis weren't able to listen to the embassy's internal communications.

Linge's file revealed that six years earlier he had investigated Alexander Litvinenko's murder in London, an affair connected to

Boris Berezovsky. So the odds were good that he had come to question the Russian oligarch's former bodyguard. That didn't concern the Israelis, but they distrusted Linge, who had caused them trouble in the past.

The Berezovsky affair hadn't involved any Israeli interests, so the Mossad stayed clear of it and hadn't interrogated the former bodyguard. It would have been easy to forbid Dan to talk to Linge, but the Americans would see that as an unfriendly gesture.

"Where is Linge right now?" asked Burg.

"He ate at the embassy and is back at his hotel. We bugged his room, of course."

Peretz didn't want to be caught napping.

"Two of our agents will pick him up as soon as he comes out," he continued. "We don't know where and when he'll meet Dan, because he hasn't contacted him yet."

Peretz's pager beeped, and he took out his cell phone. After a brief conversation he said:

"The schmuck just left his hotel. A guy from the embassy came to get him in his car. They're heading north. That's not where Dan lives. I wonder what they're up to?"

"We'll find out soon enough," said Burg.

The Shin Bet officer didn't like the idea of having someone like Malko Linge on the loose in Tel Aviv without knowing what he was up to.

A tall man dressed like a bum—like most Israelis, in other words—was pacing in front of the Habima Theatre. He had a weathered face and cropped gray hair.

"That's Yossi Milton," said Harding, stopping to pick him up. They drove toward the old Turkish port, which was now inhabited by Israeli Palestinians. Threading their way through the maze of busy, narrow streets was slow, but it had an advantage: it was easy to tell if you were being followed.

"So, what brings you back to Israel?" asked the *Haaretz* reporter.

"I'm here to see a former Mossad agent," said Malko. "His name is Uri Dan, and he used to work for Boris Berezovsky in London. Do you know anything about him?"

"The name doesn't ring a bell. Let me check my records."

Milton took out an iPad mini and started scrolling down the screen.

They slowly drove along a street crowded with handcarts.

"We're being followed," Harding announced, his voice loud in the silence of the car. "A tan Toyota. This is the third time I've seen it."

That didn't seem to bother Milton, who was apparently used to that sort of thing.

"Here we go . . . Uri Dan," the reporter said after a few minutes. "He was in my old files. . . . Not somebody especially important. Worked in the Institute's security service and didn't do actual intelligence work. Quit seven years ago and was immediately hired by a security company. Pretty low-level. . . . He worked in Israel for two years and was then recruited to England. This was authorized by his old bosses; they didn't know it would be to guard Berezovsky.

"From what I see here, he worked for one of Berezovsky's friends, Michael Cherney. Probably the guy who recommended him. I don't have Dan's current address. He's not a major figure."

"We have the address," said Malko. "Is that all you have?"

"'Fraid so. Has he agreed to see you?"

"We haven't asked him," said Harding. "We're going there now."

The Israeli looked behind them, smiled, and said:

"You aren't going alone, apparently. Our friends don't like letting you out of their sight. Which way are you driving?"

"Brodsky Street," said Harding.

"You can drop me off at a bus stop. I'm going back to the paper."

Brodsky Street was quiet, far from Tel Aviv's busy downtown. It almost looked like a street in Provence. Checking the house numbers as they passed, Harding stopped in front of a modern, expensive-looking three-story building.

"Here we are," he said.

The two men got out, and the young American studied the Hebrew names on the mailboxes.

"He's on the second floor."

The building's front door didn't have a digital lock, so they were able to walk right in. No elevator, either.

"Apartment Six," said the American.

They rang the bell and waited, holding their breath.

There were sounds from within, and the door opened to reveal a tall, athletic man with a shaved head. The look he gave them was cold, almost transparent. He quickly sized up his two visitors and asked a question in Hebrew.

Harding answered, explaining the reason for their visit. Dan listened, impassive, then turned to Malko.

"You came all the way from London to see me?" he asked in perfect English, with a note of surprise. "Why not see me there?"

"We didn't have your address. May we come in?"

Dan hesitated only for a moment, then opened the door wide. "Come on in."

They sat down in a small, anonymous living room. To break the silence, Malko asked:

"Have you gone back to work yet?"

The Israeli shook his head, taking out a cigarette.

"No, not yet. I only just got back. I called the company I used to work for. I think they'll find me something. I've been gone a long time."

Dan's affect was studiously neutral, almost indifferent.

"How can I help you?" he asked.

"You're the person who found Mr. Berezovsky's body," said Malko.

"That's right."

"What condition was it in?"

"It's in the police report: lying on the floor with a cord around his neck. The other end was tied to the showerhead."

"Was he dead?"

"Yes, more than an hour. Rigor mortis had already set in."

Dan was answering in a neutral tone, as if it was none of his concern. Malko decided to press him:

"Many people think Mr. Berezovsky didn't kill himself. Given the position of the body, do you think it was really suicide?"

Dan gave him a very slight, vague smile.

"That's a question you'd have to ask the British police. I'm not a forensics expert."

"But you must have an opinion."

A long silence followed, eventually broken by Dan. With a cool glance at Malko, he calmly said:

"I signed an affidavit for the local police swearing not to speak to anyone about this affair, because the investigation is still open. I can't tell you anything else."

"Not even your opinion?"

Dan didn't bother answering, just stubbed out his cigarette in an ashtray and stood up.

"As I said, I can't tell you anything else. Since you're with an official American agency, you should contact Scotland Yard."

He politely saw them out, gave them a perfunctory handshake, and quietly shut the door.

The man was as smooth as a stone.

Harding waited until they were downstairs before asking:

"So what do you think?"

Malko smiled bitterly.

"We just got proof of the collusion between the British and the Russians. They don't want this story getting out.

"The Brits put the squeeze on Dan to keep him quiet. A bodyguard is easy to pressure. He has to think of his future, in case he wants to go back to England. I'm sure Dan could have told us something if he were willing to talk. He's the only person who could say if the suicide looked suspicious, and he clearly isn't about to."

When they came out, the tan Toyota was parked some distance away, but it didn't follow them. Uri Dan was about to have more visitors.

Hearing Malko's account, Snow looked disappointed.

"Do you think the Israelis got to him?" asked the station chief.

"They didn't have to," said Malko. "Dan was already programmed by the time he left London. The English shut him up to make sure he didn't say anything."

"So what does this tell you?"

"It confirms what we already suspected, a secret agreement between the British and the Russians. The prime minister gets reconciliation and a business deal. In exchange, he wipes the slate clean of the Litvinenko and Berezovsky affairs. There won't be any inquiry, the suicide thesis becomes the official story, and any possible investigation will be blocked."

"That's crappy!" said Snow.

"And worrisome," added Malko. "You have to wonder how far this Russo-British rapprochement will go."

A hush descended on the two men—accompanied by the ghosts of Burgess and Maclean.

The CIA had never completely recovered from the Cambridge Five episode, in which their closest ally had made a pact with the devil. With the Cold War heating up again, they now had to determine the extent of the rot.

"So what do you plan to do now?" asked Snow.

"Leave Israel. There's nothing else for me to do here."

"To go where?"

"That's a good question," said Malko. "I still want to prove that Berezovsky was killed, but I need evidence. I have a lead in London, but I don't know where it will take me."

"You should drop the case," said the station chief. "It's hopeless. Sounds as if the Russians and the British have done a complete lockdown."

"Well, we'll try to spring some of the locks," said Malko. "Plus, I have a personal score to settle. The Russians tried to kill me. I know the man who did it, and I think he's still in London."

Malko knew that the key to the affair could only be in one of two places: London or Moscow. The order to assassinate Berezovsky had come from Moscow. But whom could he see there who could help him?

If he went to Moscow, the Russians would immediately know why and might react. They didn't want the oligarch's death to be aired.

Either way, Malko would again be playing Russian roulette if he continued.

The problem was, he was in no mood to quit.

CHAPTER

10

The small office at MI5 headquarters was lit by a window with a view of the Thames below and a gray sky above. The four-person meeting was chaired by William Sharp, the senior Service official who handled cases that required absolute secrecy.

"What's the latest, Luke?" he asked, turning to the man on his right.

Luke Selinger was the coordinator of information regarding Boris Berezovsky's death. He had received the results of the Surrey Police inquiry, the bodyguard's statement, and the investigation evidence, including forensic samples from the body. And as ordered, he had authorized the Russian oligarch's burial three weeks after his death.

Selinger opened the file in front of him.

"Special Branch sent me a report on an incident at the Lanesborough that might be relevant to the matter I'm handling now," he said.

"How so?" asked Sharp.

"It involves a very strange death. Three days ago, a Pakistani chambermaid named Benazir Saldo fell ill while she was cleaning one of the rooms, number 418. She was found unconscious, in very bad physical shape. She was taken to hospital and died several hours later.

"The cause of death wasn't immediately obvious, except that it involved nervous system failure. Her pupils were constricted to pinpoints, as if she'd been given a massive dose of atropine.

"Given the unusual symptoms, the coroner called on the poison specialists of St. Mary's Hospital, where the body was taken. They gave Special Branch their conclusions the next day. Ms. Saldo apparently died after inhaling a poison gas, like sarin or soman, which causes death very quickly."

Sharp's eyebrows shot up.

"Tell me more about these gases," he said.

"They are organophosphates similar to the poison gases used in World War I, sir. When inhaled, a milligram is enough to kill a man. The cult Aum Shinrikyo released sarin gas in the Tokyo subway in 1995, killing thirteen people."

The MI5 official looked shocked.

"Who in heaven's name is still using poison gas?"

Selinger paused before answering.

"The gases have been used in Syria recently, by both sides, sir. But we've never seen a case like this in Britain before. These substances are only produced by the defense industry. It's practically impossible for an ordinary criminal to obtain them."

"Do we ourselves have a supply?" asked Sharp.

"I don't know, sir. That would be a military secret."

"So who can get their hands on them?"

Selinger cleared his throat.

"Only a major intelligence service with the support of its government, sir."

A hush descended on the room. Why would an intelligence agency want to kill a Pakistani chambermaid?

Sharp broke the silence again.

"Is that all you have, Luke?"

"No, sir. After sending the report, Special Branch conducted an in-depth investigation at the Lanesborough. They sent me their conclusions this morning.

"The maid cleaning the room spotted some currency in the closet safe that the guest must have forgotten. Per regulations, she immediately called security so they could come get the money. To do that, she used the room phone.

"When security personnel arrived a few minutes later, she was already unconscious, but the sequence of events was clear.

"Needless to say, Special Branch impounded the telephone and tested it. Traces of soman were found on the plastic handset. Someone had entered the room and smeared or dripped it onto the handset. Whoever used the phone next would inhale the gas. However, it seems unlikely that the target was an ordinary chambermaid, and—"

Sharp interrupted:

"Who was staying in that room?"

"An Austrian citizen named Malko Linge," Selinger promptly answered. "He had been at the Lanesborough for a week."

"Do you have anything on him?"

"Yes, sir, we know him very well. Linge is a CIA operative who has often traveled to London, notably for the Litvinenko affair seven years ago. He checked out of the hotel that morning to travel to Tel Aviv."

The silence that followed could be cut with a knife.

"So he could have been the target of the attack," said Sharp.

"It's likely, sir. That's the conclusion we reached, but we can't prove it."

William Sharp didn't need proof. In a case like this, there was only one possible responsible party: the Russian secret services, those veteran poisoners. But why attack Malko Linge here? he wondered. They could just as easily kill him in Austria or anywhere else.

"Do we know what Linge was doing in London?" he asked.

"No, sir. Given the timing, we suspect he came to investigate Boris Berezovsky's death, but that's just a theory."

New silence.

"Who knows about this business?"

"No one outside of the investigation," said Selinger. "Special Branch ordered the Lanesborough staff to keep absolutely quiet about the incident. News of it hasn't reached the press. The maid's family was told she died of heart failure, so there's no problem on that side.

"I requested this meeting so I could receive your instructions, sir. This is a case of attempted murder of a member of a sister organization. The Agency isn't aware of it, since the target was missed. Should we notify them?"

"No, you shouldn't," said Sharp crisply. "This case must remain top secret. I will refer it to the director general, who will decide. Include this material in the Berezovsky file. I assume Special Branch hasn't identified a suspect?"

"No one knows who entered the room, or how," said Selinger. "They were obviously professionals and needed only a few minutes. Every service knows how to open a magnetic lock without leaving traces."

"Very well," concluded Sharp. "Keep me apprised of any developments."

Stanley Dexter was feeling somewhat intimidated as he pushed open the door to the Travellers Club. The CIA station chief had been invited to the club only twice since being posted to London. One of the most exclusive gentlemen's clubs in the capital, the Travellers was used by senior British officials for confidential meetings. Outsiders were not welcome.

That morning, a messenger had hand-delivered a note from Sir George Dearlove, inviting him to lunch there at twelve thirty. Dexter was intrigued. This wasn't their usual way to communicate, and the MI5 director general wasn't in the habit of lunching with an ordinary CIA station chief.

As Dexter entered, a steward in a morning suit appeared out of nowhere. With a cool but affable smile, he asked:

"Are you a member of the club, sir?"

It was a pro forma question, since he knew them all, but a polite way of excluding the great unwashed.

"No, I'm not. Sir George Dearlove invited me."

"Perfect!" said the steward, his smile widening. "Kindly follow me, please!"

As they walked, he quickly checked his lunch list and led Dexter to one of the club's small dining rooms, the one with red velvet wallpaper, and seated him at a table

"I wish you an excellent lunch, sir," he said, and disappeared.

A few moments later, a waiter brought some cucumber sandwiches and bottled water and asked Dexter if he wanted a drink. The station chief said no.

The silence in the little dining room was so total, you would've thought you were in a crypt, far from the noise of London. Yet Piccadilly was just a few hundred yards away.

As Dexter absentmindedly took one of the sandwiches, he wondered what the MI5 chief could possibly want with him. It was a sign of favor to be invited to the Travellers, so it had to be something positive.

Dexter was drinking a scotch and finishing the last of the sandwiches when the tall, ascetic figure of Sir George Dearlove appeared. Dexter had an excuse for eating the sandwiches: it was already one thirty. The MI5 chief sat down at the table and apologized.

"I'm terribly sorry! I was called to a cabinet meeting that ran late. I hope they've been taking good care of you."

"Perfectly," said Dexter.

A maître d' brought the day's menu, which was very simple: asparagus au gratin, lamb chops, and dessert. Dexter wasn't optimistic about dessert, feeling as he did that English pastry was still in the Stone Age—cinder-block-like cakes, oddly hued custards, and very strange fruit tarts.

Dearlove ordered a gin and tonic to keep Dexter's scotch company. They clinked glasses and made the requisite small talk about the weather—terrible, as usual. Then the MI5 chief said:

"You must be wondering about the reason for this lunch."

"I'm always pleased to see you, Sir George, and this place is delightful."

"My dear fellow, this isn't a social invitation," Dearlove said with a smile. "Our meeting must remain secret from both our houses. That's why I used a messenger. All my phone calls are recorded."

"But you're the director general!"

"That's true, but we have a very efficient internal security system. Besides, I'm merely a senior official in Her Majesty's service. I obey the political powers that be."

Dexter nodded, but without understanding.

The asparagus arrived, and with it, a break in the conversation. They were alone in the small dining room. When Dearlove finished his asparagus, he said quietly:

"I am here without my government's or my service's knowledge. What I'm about to tell you might be considered treason because I am going against my government's orders. Orders that were given to me only orally. If word of this meeting gets out, I will be immediately dismissed and lose much else besides. Can you promise me that this conversation will not be reported to anyone?"

"Not even Langley?"

"Not for the time being, because Langley is also accountable to the political leadership. We have no way of knowing into whose ears the information I'm going to give you might fall."

"Very well, I agree," said Dexter, who by now was dying to know more. Why all the mystery? he wondered. The man sitting across from him wasn't given to joking.

"So what do you want to tell me?"

Dropping his voice even lower, Dearlove said:

"I believe Malko Linge, one of your operatives, spent some time in London recently."

"That's right."

"He was the object of a murder attempt that failed. A deadly poison was put on the telephone in his room at the Lanesborough. Luckily for him, he didn't use it, and a Pakistani chambermaid died instead. Mr. Linge doesn't know this because he had already left the hotel at the time.

"When I heard about the poisoning, I immediately decided to tell you. But before contacting the Agency officially, I asked Downing Street for clearance. It was denied.

"The British government does not want you to be informed of this incident."

CHAPTER

11

The CIA station chief looked so dumbfounded, Dearlove couldn't help but smile.

"That's why I've become a Deep Throat," he said. "Because of the way I see my job. I'm not a politician. Our two services are allies, fighting the same enemies. And you've always stood by us, even during the terrible Burgess-Maclean period in the fifties."

"Thank you," said Dexter in a dull voice. "Who gave you that order, Sir George, and why?"

"It came from the prime minister himself. It's the outcome of a deal between David Cameron and Vladimir Putin, struck when he came to London last year. A political deal, the details of which I don't know."

Dearlove went on to explain that relations with Russia had been in a deep freeze since 2003, when Britain granted political asylum to Boris Berezovsky.

"The polonium was tracked back to Moscow. We even learned the name of the man who brought it to England: Andrey Lugovoy, an ex-FSB agent who later became a member of the Duma. He could only have gotten it from the GRU."

The chill between the two countries lasted until the majority in the House of Commons changed.

"When David Cameron became PM, he decided for business

reasons to make peace with President Putin and invited him to London," said the MI5 chief. "Nobody knows exactly what the two men agreed on, but we won the right to provide security for the 2014 Sochi Olympics right after that visit, as well as other commercial accords."

Dearlove paused for a sip of his drink before continuing.

"Here are two facts I find deeply troubling," he said.

"Fact one: a few months after President Putin's visit, a judge on the Litvinenko case was ordered not to reveal certain evidence that implicated Russia in the murder. The order was a political one, and it came from Ten Downing Street.

"Fact two: Boris Berezovsky inexplicably lost his lawsuit against Roman Abramovich over ownership of the Russian oil company Sibneft. A British court ruled that he'd never owned shares in the company, which flies in the face of the evidence."

"That's certainly disturbing, Sir George, but it's understandable," said Dexter, who knew all this already. "Maybe even acceptable, to some degree."

"True enough," said Dearlove. "MI5 wasn't involved, so we took no action. But then came Berezovsky's death, the so-called suicide. That happened a little more than a month ago, as you know. Everyone, including his friends, claimed it was a sophisticated killing by the Kremlin. Everyone, that is, except the British police. We didn't have jurisdiction, so the local police investigated and sent their report to Scotland Yard. To date, they have refused to share it with us.

"There was no real investigation. The forensic samples weren't tested, and the police allowed Berezovsky to be buried without a real autopsy being conducted.

"Within the Service, we concluded that Berezovsky's death was part of a deal between Putin and the PM, and it concluded an affair that was very touchy for the Russians. Reasons of state, you know. After all, few people outside of Berezovsky's family really mourned him. For us, the case was closed. Until what happened at the Lanesborough."

Dearlove paused for breath, then said:

"I have to ask you a question: Was your man Linge working on Berezovsky's death?"

"Yes, he was. That's why he was in London. But he hasn't turned up anything yet."

The MI5 chief looked visibly relieved.

"So I haven't betrayed my service for nothing," he said. "It means the Russians tried to eliminate Mr. Linge to stop his investigation. Which makes sense in a way, but it also proves that Berezovsky didn't kill himself. If there hadn't been anything to uncover, they wouldn't have attempted the murder."

"Thank you for telling me about this," said Dexter. "It's an extremely kind gesture. And very useful."

"I'm on the horns of a dilemma," Dearlove admitted. "I understand the PM's political motivation. Reasons of state take precedence over individual cases. But as the head of MI5, I can't abide the idea of my political leaders letting people who aren't our friends kill someone on British soil. That's why I wanted to alert you. I was given a political order not to pursue the matter of the poisoning attempt, but I refuse to follow it."

Just then, a waiter came in with coffee and dessert, and the two men stopped talking.

After their coffee, Dearlove looked at his watch.

"I'm going to have to leave you," he said. "I'm counting on your absolute discretion, Mr. Dexter. I've put my fate in your hands, but there are some things I simply won't stand for."

"I won't forget this, Sir George. Do I have your permission to inform Malko himself?"

"Yes, of course, though I think he would do well to return to his castle in Austria for now."

The two men exchanged a lengthy handshake, and Dexter watched the tall Englishman walk away. What Sir George Dearlove didn't know was that the Lanesborough poisoning wasn't the first attempt on Malko's life to stop his investigation, but the second.

When Malko awoke in his room at the Dan Hotel, he was greeted with the sight of a cloudless blue sky and people cavorting on the beach below, but the taste in his mouth was sour. His whole Israel expedition was a fiasco. The British had gotten to the bodyguard, who clearly wasn't about to tell him anything.

After a shower, Malko decided to chance sending a text to Gwyneth. He made it as neutral as possible:

Anything new?

The reply arrived moments later and was just as brief:

Not yet.

With his investigation in London stalled, Malko figured he might as well go back to Austria. It would give Gwyneth time to pump her source for more information. He was about to ask the front desk about flights to Vienna when he got a second text:

I must see you. It's important. Stanley.

So he would have to go back through London after all. Maybe when he saw Gwyneth he would learn something from her in person, he thought. But what could the CIA station chief want with him?

It was a sign of Rem Tolkachev's trust in Boris Tavetnoy of the London FSB *rezidentura* that he had been made the liaison with the cell in charge of the Berezovsky case, including doping the phone at the Lanesborough. So when Malko Linge left London for Israel, still alive and well, Tavetnoy started quaking in his boots.

Yet nothing untoward seemed to have happened. The Russian eagerly perused all the newspapers but found no mention of a poisoning at the hotel. Either the nerve agent had dissipated naturally, or it had somehow been neutralized. Nor was there any reaction from Scotland Yard or MI5. And since Linge had left England, the case seemed to be closed.

It was on that optimistic note that Tavetnoy ended his message to the spymaster in Moscow: the Berezovsky case was finally concluded, and Russia wouldn't be implicated.

Sitting in the CIA station chief's office, Malko listened to Stanley Dexter's account of the Lanesborough poisoning in slack-jawed astonishment. Malko hadn't turned up anything new in the Berezovsky case, yet the Russians were apparently still after him, and in a particularly vicious and sophisticated way. It had already cost an innocent Pakistani chambermaid her life.

Was it to keep him from meeting the bodyguard? Malko wondered. His visit to Tel Aviv proved that wasn't the case. Unless the Russians didn't know that the British had already silenced Dan. Only one conclusion was possible.

"We can now be pretty certain that Berezovsky was assassinated," he said. "Otherwise the FSB wouldn't be going to such lengths to stop my investigation."

"Which hasn't produced anything so far," the station chief pointed out.

"I still have one more lead," said Malko shortly, "but it's a long shot, and I can't tell you about it yet."

Dexter shook his head.

"I think you've taken enough chances," he said. "I'm going to suggest to Langley that we shut down this operation. There's no point in your staying in London twiddling your thumbs without much hope. Let's face it: the Russians have accomplished what they set out to do."

"I don't feel like giving up," said Malko. "I still have a contact in London that might pay off. Also, I thought of something that might take the Russians by surprise."

"What's that?"

"Going to Moscow."

The CIA station chief stared at him in amazement.

"You're crazy!" he cried. "They've already tried to kill you here in London. In Moscow, nothing will stop them!"

"It's a risk," Malko admitted, "but it might kick over the anthill. The FSB would be caught flat-footed, and they might make a mistake. I'm sure all this is coming out of Moscow, so that's where to find the people behind it."

"Do you know any of those people?"

"I might."

"Who do you have in mind?"

"An old girlfriend of Litvinenko's named Irina Lopukin. I met her at his funeral. She's divorced from her banker husband, who gave her a lot of money. When I talked to her in London she seemed very well informed about the ins and outs of this affair. She's angry at the people who killed Litvinenko, so she might be willing to help."

"You could be putting her in danger."

"Irina can take care of herself. She knows her way around the corridors of power, and she knows about Lugovoy. When she was dating Litvinenko, he was still an FSB agent, remember. She also has very high-level political connections."

"You're taking a pretty big chance," said Dexter.

"Maybe, but I've thought of something that might help. I'm going to go to Vienna and ask the station chief there to send me to Moscow officially, to investigate the Edward Snowden affair. I'll even pay the Moscow FSB a formal visit. It might throw them off the track."

"I doubt it," said Dexter. "But I'll forward your proposal to Langley. Are you going back to the Lanesborough?"

"Why not?" said Malko with a smile. "The Russians don't know I've returned to London, unless the Brits told them, which I doubt. And they can't booby-trap *all* the rooms. Let me know when you get Langley's answer."

Despite his bravado, Malko felt odd to be back at the Lanesborough, in a room identical to the one whose telephone the FSB had poisoned. Good thing he wasn't superstitious.

Still, he felt a bit on edge when he called Gwyneth Robertson. She answered almost immediately.

"Are you still in Tel Aviv?"

"No, I'm in London. I'd like to see you."

"I can't this evening—because of you, incidentally. But I can swing by the hotel tomorrow morning."

"I'll be waiting," said Malko.

CHAPTER

12

Malko started when his room phone rang. Repressing a twinge of apprehension, he picked up the handset.

"I'm downstairs," said Gwyneth Robertson brightly.

"Aren't you coming up?" he asked. "We can have a room service breakfast."

"Don't tempt me! I haven't much time, and I know how easily I melt. I'll be waiting in the lounge."

Malko didn't insist. Downstairs, he found the young American in one of the small rooms off the bar. She had already ordered them breakfast. In her silk suit, nude stockings, and high heels, Gwyneth was as sexy as ever. Sensing Malko's eyes on her, she looked up and smiled.

"So, did you find any beautiful Israeli women in Tel Aviv?"

"I didn't find much of anything at all," said Malko irritably.

When he told her what happened with Berezovsky's bodyguard, she nodded soberly.

"I'm not surprised. We've stumbled into an international political and economic deal. I'm reminded of it every day."

"By your friend James?"

"Yeah, but he's stonewalling me. In a normal situation, I'd have gotten him to spill the beans a long time ago. Problem is, this Arkady Lianin guy is up to his neck in the Berezovsky affair. James hinted that if word got out that he was helping me find him, he'd be risking his career, and maybe more."

A waiter brought orange juice, tea, coffee, toast, and scrambled eggs. When he left, Malko said:

"Listen, Gwyn, why don't you just drop it? I'm sorry I asked you to do this. You aren't going to be able to pull it off."

The former CIA case officer gave him an almost sadistic smile.

"Oh, yes I will! James is completely hooked, so now I'll put him on half rations until he gives in. He's nuts about me. Calls me all day long, constantly texts, even talks about getting divorced. If I pull back a little now, he'll go out of his mind."

Malko gazed at her thoughtfully. Gwyneth was prostituting herself for him, and doing it out of affection and complicity. In his mind's eye, Malko imagined her having sex with the young MI5 officer. It wasn't an especially pleasant thought.

"It may take a little longer, but he's going to give me *something*," she said. "Either that, or I'm losing my touch."

"That is definitely not the case," Malko assured her.

Straightening up in her chair, she crossed her legs very high, revealing expanses of her stockinged thighs. Gwyneth always seemed ready to fuck or be fucked. As she buttered her toast, she gave him some advice.

"There's no point in your waiting here in London," she said. "You're certainly under surveillance, and if the Russians see you hanging around, they'll wonder why. Go back to Liezen! I'll contact you as soon as I get what I want."

"I'm planning to leave London all right, but I'm not going home."

"Really? Where are you off to?"

"Moscow."

"You're nuts!" she snapped, putting her toast down. "Do you have a death wish, or what? The FSB hates your guts. They've already tried to kill you a couple of times. They even tried here not that long ago, as I recall. What the hell are you going to do in Moscow, anyway?"

"Pull the lion's tail," said Malko with a smile. "Everything started with Moscow, and I have some contacts there. My showing up might rattle the FSB and cause them to make a mistake."

"You're the one making the mistake," she said. "You could disappear without a trace."

"I can't stand sitting around doing nothing. And I really want to crack this case, find out exactly how the FSB managed to kill Berezovsky. Anyway, I didn't learn anything in Tel Aviv. The same thing might happen in Moscow."

"Except that in Tel Aviv you weren't in danger of being killed. Just quit the damn project!"

"I won't," said Malko, shaking his head. "Anyway, you know I like to play Russian roulette."

"Yeah, but in this case, it's Belgian roulette," she said sarcastically. "You know, with six bullets in the barrel."

They gazed at each other for a moment. Then Gwyneth took out her cell and made a brief call. Malko could hear her say: "I'll be late."

She put away the phone and gave him a mysterious smile.

"I've got half an hour free for you. Come on!"

She was already on her feet and heading for the elevator. In the car she gave Malko a long look and said:

"I don't know if I'll ever see you again. I want something to remember you by."

Gwyneth had taken off just her suit jacket and panties. Heavy breasts swinging inside her blouse, she was kneeling on the bed, giving Malko one of her patented blow jobs. When she felt he was ready, she slumped back onto the bed, flung out her arms, and said:

"Okay, let me have it."

Malko lay down on top of her, and she spread her thighs wide to ease him inside. The lack of foreplay made them both a little tense, but Malko's reluctance vanished when he felt Gwyneth's hips begin to sway. The sex wasn't a formality, either. It was a loving gesture, an emotional connection.

They made love for a long time. Panting slightly, Gwyneth gripped his shoulders at the end, and when Malko came inside her, she arched her back and gave a muffled sigh. They stayed that way for a while, at peace.

Finally she spoke.

"I hope my hunch is wrong," she said quietly. "I'd be very sad if you disappeared forever."

For Malko, the rest of the morning seemed to drag by. He had booked a flight to Vienna and was waiting to get the green light from Stanley Dexter. Finally, at two o'clock, the CIA station chief sent him a text:

Come to Grosvenor Square.

He couldn't help but feel tense when he entered the station chief's office. Dexter looked up at him with a serious expression on his face.

"I just got Langley's answer," he said. "They've approved your request to go to Moscow in spite of my negative recommendation. The Moscow station will alert the FSB that you're in town to investigate the Snowden affair. Vienna will submit your visa request. That's the best we can do, but it isn't much. You realize you're walking into the lion's den, don't you?"

"I know, but I think the game is worth the candle. Irina Lopukin could be helpful, and she's very well connected."

"From your mouth to God's ear, Malko. You know how vicious those Russians are. They'd be delighted to get rid of you, quite aside from the Berezovsky business."

"I'll take that chance. And I'll be careful."

To Malko's surprise, when he returned to Austria, his fiancée, Alexandra, wasn't at her estate. When he finally reached her by phone, he learned she was spending a few days in Croatia with friends.

"I wasn't expecting you," she said, "otherwise I wouldn't have gone. I'll be back in two days."

"I will have left by then."

"Where are you going?"

"I can't tell you. But I won't be away long."

After a short pause, Alexandra said, in a more serious tone:

"I hope you won't be taking any stupid chances."

"Don't worry. I'm going to a civilized country!"

Served by his butler, Elko Krisantem, Malko ate alone in the big dining room, then went to bed. Liezen Castle felt empty, and he didn't feel like lingering.

He got up early the next day and drove to the American embassy in Vienna. After lunch at the Hotel Sacher's Rote Bar, surrounded by gray-haired Viennese, he picked up his passport with its new Russian visa. The station chief's request had gone through smoothly. Relations between Russia and the United States might be at a low ebb, but the diplomatic niceties were still being observed. Just the same, Malko was aware that the FSB now knew he was coming to Moscow.

An impassive immigration officer at Sheremetyevo Airport stamped Malko's passport, and he walked though the busy new terminal. Outside, the usual scrum of taxis awaited. Malko was bargaining with five cab drivers who were competing to drive him into town for an outrageous price when he spotted a young man holding a sign with his name on it.

Malko went over and identified himself.

"Good morning sir, I'm Foster Steele from the embassy. We reserved a room for you at the Ritz-Carlton. Will that suit you?"

"Perfectly."

The two men walked to the parking lot and drove out onto interminable Leningradsky Prospekt. The landscape hadn't changed since his last visit to Moscow, thought Malko, wondering if they were being followed. He hoped his arrival would feel like a thorn in the FSB's side.

It took them half an hour to get to the hotel, which was as flashy and lively as always.

A couple of Orthodox priests were chatting in a corner while ogling the long legs of some young call girls perched on sofas near the elevator. One of the girls on the prowl had especially attractive eyes: very pale green, underscored with a dash of black eyeliner.

In his room, Malko checked his address book for Irina Lopukin's number and then dialed.

It was a long shot, he realized. Irina might well not be in Moscow, or might not feel like talking to him. After all, they hadn't seen each other in seven years, and a lot could have happened in the interval. The phone rang for a long time, but was eventually answered.

"Who's calling?" asked a woman in Russian. It was a voice Malko immediately recognized.

"Hello, Irina, it's Linge, Malko Linge. Do you remember me?"

There was a brief silence, then she said:

"Malko! What a surprise! Where are you?"

"In Moscow. I just arrived, and you're the first person I called. I have a very fond memory of our meeting in London, even though it happened under sad circumstances."

"I do too," said the young woman. "You're lucky to catch me. I just came back from a long trip in the East. I was in Vladivostok researching real-estate investments."

"I'm happy you're back. Can I take you out to dinner?"

Another silence followed.

"There must be some new restaurants in Moscow," he persisted.

"Thanks, but I'd rather eat at home. I'm quite tired, and my housekeeper is a very good cook. Why don't you come for tea instead, around six o'clock? Do you still have the address?"

"Yes, I do."

"The apartment is number 1276. The doorman will show you the way."

When Malko hung up, he felt considerably deflated. Was he going to draw a blank with Irina Lopukin the way he had with Uri Dan? Maybe he had traveled to Moscow for nothing.

Coming out of the Ritz-Carlton, Malko took a few steps along Tverskaya Ulitsa, ignoring the limousines parked under the awning. Their drivers almost certainly worked for the FSB. The security services probably knew that Malko was in Moscow, but there was no point in making their work easier.

Instead, he flagged down a passing gray BMW. When the driver rolled down his window, Malko said:

"I'm going to the Vysokta on Kotelnicheskaya Embankment. How much would that be?"

"Five hundred rubles."

Malko got in front with the driver, and they headed toward Manezh Square, then around Red Square.

Located on the north shore of the Moskva River, Irina's building was one of Stalin's seven *vysokti* skyscrapers, built in the 1940s and early 1950s under the supervision of Lavrenty Pavlovich. Like the others, it was an enormous wedding cake with towers and terraces, in a vaguely Art Deco style—and one of Moscow's most desirable addresses.

The BMW driver dropped Malko opposite the Vysokta's main entrance and took off. They hadn't exchanged a word during the trip.

A doorman wearing as much gold braid as an admiral gave Malko a welcoming smile.

"Gospazha Irina Lopukin?" Malko asked in Russian.

"Is she expecting you, sir?"

"Yes, she is."

The man picked up an inside phone, had a brief conversation, and directed Malko to the left-hand elevator.

"Sixteenth floor, sir, apartment 1276," he said. "It's on your left as you get out of the elevator."

The hallways were enormous, their dimensions impressive. When Malko rang the bell at Irina Lopukin's apartment, he felt a little anxious. What would she look like after so many years?

When the door silently opened, Malko was met by a pair of beautiful almond-shaped green eyes. Irina was wearing her black hair in a somewhat old-fashioned braid, but her large, carefully made-up mouth glowed like a red beacon on her face.

They gazed at each other for a few moments in silence. She was still extremely good-looking, thought Malko.

Smiling warmly, she opened the door wide.

"Welcome to Moscow. I didn't think I'd ever see you again."

"Neither did I, but I'm delighted to be wrong."

"Please, come in."

He followed her into a huge, high-ceilinged living room with a view of the Moskva River. Classical music was playing on a stereo and a smell of incense hung in the air. The impeccable décor included an array of carpets, antique furniture, and paintings.

A very classy apartment.

Irina sat down on a long mauve sofa and waved Malko to a chair opposite. They were keeping things strictly professional and hadn't hugged or kissed, though he hadn't forgotten the brief encounter that brought them together seven years earlier. When he'd taken her back to the Lanesborough, he discovered an extremely sensuous woman but one firmly determined to stay in control. She hadn't let him make love to her.

The young woman now facing him seemed to have completely forgotten that fervid episode. She was sitting several feet away, on the other side of the coffee table, observing him like a cat.

A dark-haired maid appeared with a tray of tea and cakes, and served them. Irina waited for her to leave before speaking

"What brings you to Moscow, Mr. Linge?" she asked politely.

She hadn't called him Malko, he noticed, deliberately maintaining some distance between them. He hesitated before answering, but figured she was too sharp to be easily misled.

"I'm looking into Boris Berezovsky's death," he said. "I think some of the keys to the affair are here in Moscow."

Irina smiled slightly.

"In Moscow, certainly, but why here, at my place?"

Malko poured himself some tea.

"When I met you in London at Alexander Litvinenko's funeral, you said you'd made the trip especially from Moscow to attend. You also told me many things about the poisoning. You seem to be well connected with people in the FSB and those who were pulling the strings. So I thought I would come and talk to you."

Irina waited a few moments before answering. When she did, she sounded serious.

"I came to say good-bye to a man who had mattered a great deal in my life. Alexander did some big favors for me, and it's partly thanks to him that I'm able to lead a comfortable life in Moscow.

"Leonid, my husband at the time, was being pursued by Chechens and other people even more dangerous. Alexander persuaded him to put some of his assets in my name, which he could easily afford. I fell in love with Alexander. He was a very nice, gentle man. Also, he didn't drink. Leonid would start hitting the vodka at nine o'clock in the morning.

"Besides that, Alexander respected me. That's why I attended his funeral. And I haven't forgotten him. I regularly have flowers put on his grave in Highgate Cemetery."

"What did you think about Berezovsky's death?" asked Malko.

Irina sipped her tea before answering.

"He was a rat, and many people were glad to see him dead," she said with a scornful grimace. "He didn't have any heart. He's a person of no interest to me."

"Aren't you intrigued by his death?"

She gave a mirthless laugh.

"Why should I be? It's an open secret. All of Russia knows that Vladimir Putin is behind it, but nobody cares. Do you?"

"I wouldn't have mourned him," Malko admitted, "but the CIA asked me to look into his death."

"Forget it," she exclaimed. "Let him rot in his coffin!"

Irina seemed honestly indifferent to Berezovsky's fate. Thrown off balance, Malko tried for an opening.

"I don't know many people who could help me," he said. "That's why I thought of you."

A long silence followed, broken by Irina.

"I'm afraid you're on the wrong track, for two reasons. First, Berezovsky doesn't interest me: he was a predator who stole everything he could get his hands on, and we never even met. I suppose I could get some information about him, but I'm not eager to.

"The second reason is more important. I have a very pleasant life here. I spend weekends at my dacha, I go out, I have friends and a comfortable apartment. I don't want to lose all that."

"Why would you lose it?"

Irina gave him a pitying look.

"The FSB already knows that you've come to see me. The Berezovsky case is extremely sensitive. Putin may be pleased at having eliminated him, but he doesn't want the secret services blamed for it. I've heard some talk on the subject.

"If I cooperated with you, I would risk paying a very high price. Since separating from my husband, I no longer have a *kricha*— a protector.

"So I wish you good luck, but don't come see me again. Personally, I would've enjoyed it very much, but I have to think of my safety."

This came as a shock. Malko had forgotten how ferocious Russian mores could be. But Irina was right. You couldn't fight the "vertical structure." Or, if you did, there was no telling what might happen to you.

He was still mulling this over when she stood up and said simply:

"I have to get ready for my dinner."

It was without room for appeal. She walked him to the door. In seeing him out, she leaned close and kissed him lightly on the mouth.

"Good-bye," she said. "Maybe some other time, some other place."

The door closed behind him, and Malko walked toward the elevator. He hadn't expected this kind of reception. What was he going to do in Moscow now? Feeling frustrated and disappointed, he hailed a cab and went back to his hotel.

There was still one trail left, of course: that of the *Forbes Russia* journalist Ilya Sokolov, the last person to interview Berezovsky and the man the Americans suspected of leading him into his killers' clutches.

But it was a pretty slim lead.

Malko didn't feel like spending the evening alone, so he called his old friend and lover Alina Portansky, the painter's wife. The phone rang for so long that he was about to hang up when she finally answered.

"Yes?"

"Alina! It's me, Malko."

There was a long silence, and then the young woman spoke softly:

"Malko!" she said with pleasure. "Are you in Moscow?"

"Since this morning."

"I'm happy to hear your voice."

Alina's own voice seemed altered. She sounded at a loss.

"How is Alexei?" he asked.

A few more moments of silence followed.

"He's dead," she said quietly. "Six months ago. Cancer. But it was fast, and he didn't suffer too much. It made me very sad. He was a good man. And it's hard to live alone in Moscow."

"How are you managing? Did he leave you any money?"

She laughed, almost to herself.

"He never had any! He left me two hundred paintings, and I was able to live off them for a while. After that, nothing."

Malko was sincerely saddened. Alina, who never hid her affection for him, had done him many favors, sometimes at the risk of her life.

"I'd like to see you," he said. "Let's have dinner together."

"I haven't gone out in a long time," she said. "I just don't have the heart. I'm a wreck."

"I'm coming to get you," said Malko in a voice that brooked no contradiction. "Get dressed. I'll take you to the Café Pushkin and cheer you up. I'm sad about Alexei, too."

"All right," she said with a catch in her voice. "I'll try to find something to wear."

Huddled in his Kremlin office, Rem Tolkachev was reading the latest FSB reports. It was nine o'clock at night, but he didn't feel like going home. A few days earlier the president had congratulated him on the way he'd handled the Berezovsky affair. The master of the Kremlin had scored up and down the line. He'd gotten his revenge and the Russian state hadn't been implicated, thanks to the friendly attitude of the British.

As Tolkachev leafed through the pile of reports, he found one on the CIA operative Malko Linge, who had arrived that morning at Sheremetyevo and been immediately followed. The FSB didn't know what he was doing in Moscow, but it was probably connected with Berezovsky's death.

In the last line of the report, the FSB agents handling the surveillance noted that Linge had paid a visit to the Vysokta. When questioned, the doorman said he visited a tenant named Irina Lopukin.

The name sounded vaguely familiar. Turning to his computer, Tolkachev quickly found the young woman's name. She'd been involved with Alexander Litvinenko when he was still with the FSB and probably knew a lot about that affair.

The old spymaster decided that it was best to be careful. He drafted a note for the Moscow FSB. He wanted Irina Lopukin put under close surveillance.

CHAPTER

14

To Malko, Alina Portansky looked almost translucent. Her long, somewhat old-fashioned organza dress hung on her, and her vacant eyes had dark circles under them.

Just the same, she attacked her smoked herring—a Café Pushkin specialty—with gusto. And the first glass of vodka brought some color to her cheeks.

"I'm very happy to see you," she said, putting her hand on Malko's. "I've been feeling very alone."

She seemed completely detached from her sexuality, though she'd shown herself to be a wild woman in the past. For Malko, seeing Alina now was just a pleasant interlude. She didn't have anything to offer him in his investigation, and he certainly didn't want her running even the slightest risk. She had taken enough chances for him in the old days.

The atmosphere in the Pushkin was as lively as ever, and Alina gradually began to thaw.

"Our Russia has certainly changed," she said. "We've gone back to the days of the Soviet Union."

"Meaning what?"

"If you're against the regime, you can never say what you think in public, or to your neighbors. Vladimir Putin has re-created a kind of 'soft' totalitarianism, and there's no opposition left. But my fellow Russians don't care. So long as they have vodka, good sausages, and a dacha, they don't give a damn about politics."

"Do people here talk about Berezovsky's death?"

She shook her head.

"Hardly at all. He was just another corrupt oligarch, and people have forgotten him. A few articles claimed that after renouncing the motherland, he committed suicide because he couldn't come back to Russia.

"The Kremlin spread the word that Berezovsky had written to Putin begging for forgiveness, and that the president was prepared to give it to him.

"That's almost certainly false. Putin has gotten rid of the last oligarch to stand up to him, and he did it discreetly, using the old tried-and-true methods. Khodorkovsky is in Siberia, and the others, like Abramovich and Deripaska, crawl in his presence." She paused. "Why are you interested in Berezovsky's death?"

"It's work," said Malko. "I want to understand the operation, figure out exactly how they managed to disguise a murder as a suicide."

"You'll never do it," said Alina, shaking her head again. "They're professional killers, backed by the state. They strike and they disappear. Don't take any chances! Berezovsky wasn't worth it."

She sounded completely resigned.

As the meal went on, Alina seemed to slowly fade. When she finished her cutlets Pojarski, she smiled weakly and again put her hand on Malko's.

"I hope you don't mind, but I want to go home. It's been so long since I've been out. If you stay on in Moscow, we can meet again sometime."

"I'll see that you get home safely," he said.

Outside, he hailed a gypsy cab and gave the driver her address.

When they parted, Alina offered her lips in an almost chaste kiss, and said:

"I'm still in love with you, you know."

Irina Lopukin picked up her landline phone, thinking the front desk was calling. When she answered, a man's voice came on.

"Gospazha Lopukin?"

"Yes. Who is this?"

"Lieutenant Pavel Constantinov of the Moscow FSB."

"Why are you calling?" she asked after a moment, in a somewhat changed voice.

"I would like to meet with you on a matter of some importance."

Irina tried to stay calm.

"That's not a problem. Let me see when I can stop by your office. Where are you located?"

"At 26 Bolshaya Lubyanka Street."

One of the most sinister addresses in Moscow. For years, its cellars three levels down had echoed with the executions of deviationists.

"All right, I think that tomorrow I can—"

The FSB officer interrupted her, courteously but firmly.

"Gospazha Lopukin, this is an important matter. To spare you the inconvenience of a special trip, I've sent a staff car to pick you up. It's parked in front of your building. I would appreciate your coming downstairs so as not to keep my officers waiting."

Irina felt her cheeks burning. The man was giving her no choice: if she didn't go down, the FSB agents would come up, and the entire building would know she was having problems with the federal police.

"Very well," she said in a choked voice. "I'll come down."

Irina snatched her purse and her keys and went out, slamming the door. But her anger couldn't disguise the lump of fear in the pit of her stomach. When you went in to see the FSB, you never knew when you'd be coming out.

She spotted a black Audi under the Vysokta awning, with a police beacon on the left side of its roof. One of the two men in front promptly got out to open the door, and she climbed in the back.

A quarter of an hour later, the Audi pulled up to the metal gate at 26 Bolshaya Lubyanka. The trip had been considerably sped up by switching on the flashing light and driving in the middle of the road.

The gate silently slid aside, and the FSB agent next to the driver jumped out and opened the door for her.

"If you please, Gospazha Lopukin."

Times had changed since the arrests by the old KGB, she thought. They used to parade their suspects with their hands tied so far up their backs, it forced them to bend forward in the "chicken position" that humiliated CIA agents and delighted the Russians.

Led by the police officer, Irina passed a blank-faced guard standing at attention, crossed the lobby, and went up to the second floor.

An anonymous office lit by banks of fluorescent lights. The officer had Irina sit on a chair and left her.

She hadn't been searched and still had her cell phone. Wondering who she could call, she first thought of her ex-husband, but gave up the idea. Here, she was outside of time.

A few minutes later the door opened on a tall man with black hair and green eyes. He was dressed in civilian clothes and was carrying a folder. He sat down behind a desk and asked:

"Are you Irina Lopukin, the former wife of Leonid Lopukin?"

As if he didn't know.

"Yes, I am," she said quietly.

"I am Captain Nikolai Morozov of the Moscow FSB counterespionage section."

"I'm not a spy!" Irina immediately protested.

A faint smile played on the officer's face.

"Of course not, gospazha. Otherwise you wouldn't be here, but at Lefortovo prison."

"So what do you want with me?"

Morozov glanced at the file.

"We have received some information about you that caught our attention. The security of the state is our primary concern, as you know."

"What information?" she croaked, though she knew what the FSB man was about to say.

"We are exercising surveillance on a foreigner, an Austrian subject named Malko Linge. He is listed in our files as an enemy of the *rodina*, and he is currently in Moscow."

"If he's a spy, why did you let him enter Russia?"

Morozov remained impassive.

"Russia is a liberal country, gospazha. We have only suspicions concerning the man named Linge. Do you know him?"

The question was put without a trace of humor, and Irina nearly blew up.

"You know very well that he came to my apartment for tea yesterday afternoon. Otherwise I wouldn't be here."

"Why did he visit you?"

"He is someone I used to know. I met him in London a few years ago. He phoned and invited himself over. I hadn't expected to see him again."

The officer made a note of this, then looked up at her.

"Gospazha, do you mind my asking what you talked about? Mr. Linge stayed at your place for nearly two hours."

Taken aback, it took Irina a few moments to answer.

"Nothing important," she finally said. "We talked about life in Moscow. He wanted to take me out to dinner, but I refused."

"No political topics?"

"No."

"May I ask how you met in London, seven years ago?"

Irina only pretended to hesitate. The FSB clearly knew everything about her.

"I'd come for Alexander Litvinenko's funeral," she said. "He'd been one of your officers, and I met him while he was still with the FSB. I was very fond of him. After the funeral, I returned to Moscow."

The officer's face darkened.

"Alexander Litvinenko was a traitor!" he said in a taut voice. "Not many people regretted his death."

"Well, I did," said the young woman. "I've always felt a lot of affection for him. But it doesn't matter. He's dead. . . ."

A hush descended. Alexander Litvinenko had been killed by the FSB, possibly by friends of the very man who was now interrogating her.

Captain Morozov brushed the matter aside.

"I understand," he said. "Let's get back to Malko Linge. Do you plan to see him again?"

"I told you, no."

He nodded, then said calmly:

"We think it would be a good idea if you did."

"Why?"

"The man is a security risk. We would like to know what he's doing in Moscow. We think he trusts you, and you might be able to learn a great deal about him."

"I'm a Russian citizen, not a spy!" Irina said sharply. "I don't have to do your work for you."

The FSB captain didn't blink.

"All Russian citizens are auxiliaries of our organization," he said sententiously. "I'm not asking you to do anything shocking, just to behave as a good citizen."

Silence fell again.

Irina was tempted to storm out of the office, but that would have been foolish.

"Oh, very well," she said wearily, "I'll think about it. But I doubt he'll tell me anything."

"We'll be the judge of that," said Morozov. "Thank you in advance for your cooperation. One of our people will contact you in the coming days. I'll get your statement ready for signature. It'll only take a few minutes."

It took more than an hour.

Morozov returned with a sheaf of documents, and Irina initialed each page. Afterward, the FSB captain shook her hand warmly.

"We will drive you home now."

The same black Audi was waiting in the courtyard. When it pulled up at the Vysokta, the doorman looked at it with particular respect.

In Russia, the FSB called the shots.

Irina's head was in a whirl when she got back to her apartment. She tossed her purse onto the sofa and poured herself a glass of vodka. Flopping onto the sofa, she gulped it down.

She cursed herself for inviting Malko Linge to her apartment without first thinking how that might look to the secret services. She liked Malko and remembered their brief sexual encounter with pleasure, but she owed him nothing. And now, because of him, her life was going to change.

She already knew that her phones would be tapped and her apartment bugged. She would be under surveillance, followed and spied on.

She found herself in a dilemma. Her first impulse was to do nothing, to disobey the FSB order that she see Malko again. But she knew that if she did, they wouldn't leave her alone. They would go on the attack, accusing her of anti-civic behavior and causing her all sorts of grief.

The Russian public at large couldn't care less about the Berezovsky affair, but it mattered to the Kremlin, since the president himself was implicated. It wasn't something that would just go away.

Gradually, anger began to replace Irina's feeling of dejection. She hated those smooth, all-powerful bureaucrats who had such contempt for other people's lives, obeying only their superiors.

She took out her cell and dialed her ex-husband's number. The two of them were still on very good terms. Just hearing his familiar drawl raised her morale a bit.

"Hello, Leonid. I need to see you. When can we get together?"

"We can have lunch tomorrow. How about the Turandot at one?"

Leonid Lopukin didn't ask any questions. He was used to problems.

"I'll be there," she promised.

He would be able to advise her, she thought, but that wasn't enough. Just as she was about to make another call, she suddenly realized the situation she was in. From now on, all of her contacts would be monitored. Before taking another step, she had to get some information, find out what Malko might be after in Moscow.

Only one man could tell her that.

Her old friend Lavrenty Pavlovich now sat on the National Security Council. He was powerful enough not to be afraid of the FSB, which took orders from him. If she called on Pavlovich, the FSB would have to back off.

But she had to find a way to contact him.

Irina wrote a brief note requesting an urgent meeting, put it in an envelope, and phoned the doorman.

"I have a note to be taken to the Kremlin. Can you deliver it?"

When the doorman appeared a few minutes later, Irina told him where to deliver the envelope and gave him a five-hundred-ruble bill.

Feeling better, she sat back down on the sofa and lit a cigarette. She wasn't going to let them push her around.

Malko slouched in front of his television at the Ritz-Carlton, brooding. Alina had thanked him warmly for dinner last night, but he was no further along than before.

What should he do next?

He had to contact Washington.

Minutes later he was in a taxi bound for the American embassy, having warned station chief Roy Garden that he was on his way.

"Are things working out so far?" the CIA man asked when Malko entered his office.

"Not really. I'm going around in circles. Did you get any information here about Berezovsky's death?"

"Not much beyond rumors," said Garden, shaking his head. "Of course we're sure it was an operation run by the Kremlin."

He paused.

"Do you need a secure communication link?"

"Yes."

"I'll take you to the yellow submarine"—the only place in the embassy beyond the reach of the Russians' extremely sophisticated listening devices—he said.

When Malko was alone, he dialed Stanley Dexter's number in London. He had to report to him first.

Dexter called back a few minutes later, after stepping out of a meeting.

"Are you having problems?" he asked.

Without mentioning any names, Malko brought Dexter up to date on his current impasse, concluding:

"There's nothing left for me to do in Moscow. My only lead has gone cold."

"In that case, come home. No point wasting any more time and money. We'll just write the Berezovsky affair off as a loss. By the way, did you consider following up with the journalist?"

Malko admitted that he didn't quite know how to approach the man. Sokolov wasn't likely to welcome him with open arms, and Malko didn't have any specific questions for him.

"I'm going to give myself until tomorrow," he said. "And if nothing turns up, I'll catch a flight to Austria."

Riding in a taxi along the Koltso, Moscow's inner ring road, Malko felt bitter and discouraged. The Russians must be laughing up their sleeves, he thought. But when he got back to his hotel, he suddenly remembered his old Georgian friend Gocha Sukhumi. Gocha probably didn't have any information for him, but he was always good for a few laughs.

Though the men had had their differences, Sukhumi gave a joyous roar when he recognized Malko's voice.

"You're in town, right? I'm giving a little party at home tonight, so come. I'll be expecting you."

Sukhumi didn't even ask what Malko was doing in Moscow.

In the old days, before he got rich, Sukhumi belonged to the Georgian KGB. He'd also been close to Berezovsky and "the family" at the Kremlin. Since becoming a millionaire, Sukhumi had distanced himself from them a little, but he still had plenty of connections. Malko figured that at the very least, he had a pleasant evening in store.

Now fatter and his face redder, Sukhumi hugged Malko with all his might.

His large apartment on the bank of the Moskva River was jammed with a noisy crowd of men and women, all drinking like there was no tomorrow. In a corner, a band was playing Russian music.

"You see that little bitch over there?" asked Sukhumi quietly. He was pointing to a girl with dark hair, enormous breasts, and an ass so lovely, it could be in a museum. Her face, oddly enough, looked completely innocent.

"She looks like she could carry the icon in a church procession, right? Well, she's the most shameless slut I've ever met. She's already had the entire Dynamo football team. Her name's Nadejda. I saved her for you."

"That's nice of you, Gocha, but—"

Sukhumi frowned. "Hey, don't piss me off! I gave her ten thousand rubles, and she'll only fuck the guy I tell her to. So when you've had enough vodka, take her into the green salon and bang her lights out."

As if the girl knew she was being talked about, she turned and gave Malko a smile that held every vice in the world. Then she walked off, swinging her dreamy derrière and stiffening every man she passed.

"God, she's hot!" rumbled Sukhumi. "You're not gonna pass that up, are you?"

Malko could feel his scruples weakening.

He made his way through the crowd out to the wide terrace overlooking the Moskva. It was a warm evening, and couples were flirting here and there. He happened to find himself behind a woman in a black dress and accidentally brushed her behind. The owner of the ass turned around and caught his eye. It was Nadejda.

"Good evening," she said in a high voice. "Are you Gocha's friend?"

You got the feeling the girl was so fragile that if you touched her, she might break. Yet her breasts overflowed her dress unsupported by any bra, and her akimbo stance broadcast sexuality with a loudspeaker.

"Can I get you something to drink?" asked Malko.

"Yes, please," said Nadejda. "An orangeade."

One can't have *all* the vices.

He had almost reached the bar when he noticed a tall, slim brunette in a very low-cut black velvet leotard and a long skirt. Their eyes met. It was Irina Lopukin.

CHAPTER

15

Irina smiled first, and extended her hand to Malko.

"What a surprise!" she exclaimed. "I didn't know you knew Gocha."

"I didn't know you did either."

Just then, a husky man materialized behind her.

"This is my friend Yuri Khokhov," she said in a very worldly way.

Khokhov looked like a grizzly that had just come out of hibernation. Muttering something, he led Irina away to the other side of the terrace.

"I'll catch you later!" she called out.

Malko couldn't tell if that was conventional politeness or if it meant something more. Irina certainly hadn't encouraged him the previous evening.

He continued his progress to the bar, was served an orangeade, and returned with it to Nadejda. She hadn't budged and was using an icy stare to keep a swarm of admirers at bay.

"Thank you!" she said in her high voice.

She really was an extraordinary creature, thought Malko. A caricature of a pinup.

Suddenly Gocha Sukhumi burst from the crowd holding a black caviar sandwich in one hand and a glass of vodka in the other. Wrapping a massive arm around the girl—Malko thought he might snap her in two—he whispered something into her ear. When he walked off, Nadejda remained as impassive as before but with this difference: wherever Malko went, she followed, like a trained animal.

Nadejda was far and away the sexiest woman at the party, and Malko was getting seriously turned on.

He wandered through the various rooms of Gocha's vast apartment, with Nadejda right on his heels, like a cat. Suddenly she came close, looked him in the eye, and said:

"I'd like it if you would show me the apartment. I don't know it very well."

Without waiting for an answer, she took his hand and led him down a hallway lined with cartons of vodka and Armenian cognac.

Nadejda knew exactly where she was going.

She opened a door, and when Malko saw the green wallpaper, he knew where they were. The moment they were inside, she locked the door, then came over to Malko and drew close. With the same innocent expression on her face, she gently pressed her crotch against his.

When the tip of her tongue touched Malko's lips, he felt something like an electric shock. Playing with his tongue, Nadejda kissed him with exquisite skill.

It was almost more than he could stand.

He slipped an arm around her waist and she immediately pressed against him harder.

His hand slipped down to her incredibly curvaceous ass. It felt so bouncy and firm, it seemed almost unreal.

Wasting no time, Nadejda confidently reached for Malko's fly and started to caress him, quickly raising a monstrous erection. While telling himself that she was just an obedient little whore, all he could think of was plunging into that extraordinary rump.

With the same delicacy, Nadejda pulled Malko's cock from his alpaca trousers and stroked it for a few seconds more. Then she led him to the big green velvet sofa and knelt on it, with her back to him. Slipping a hand under her skirt, she pulled down a tiny black string panty and tossed it to the floor. Her chest braced against the cushions, she arched her back, further increasing Malko's desire.

Then, in her little-girl voice, she said:

"Go ahead!"

He had only to slip the skirt up her hips and step a little closer to put his cock against her pussy. He'd barely touched the wet warmth when he lost all restraint. He plunged into her with a powerful thrust, grabbing her ass in both hands, the better to guide himself.

Eyes closed and her head tilted to one side, the girl let him do whatever he pleased. Malko was beyond thinking. At some level he knew that this encounter was meaningless, but he'd turned into a caveman. Nadejda's amazing ass radiated a sexuality so potent that Malko's entire consciousness flooded into his dick. But even as he fucked her, he found himself imagining the next step. There was no way he would skip using her every which way.

When he slowly pulled out, Nadejda understood his intentions perfectly. With her hands she spread her ass cheeks the better to take him in.

A silent invitation.

All Malko had to do was to set his cock on the dusky ring and give a little push. Sodomy was clearly a sport Nadejda knew something about. Malko thought his head was going to explode.

Synapses overloaded, his every conscious thought lay in his cock as it penetrated that astonishing ass.

As Malko felt his orgasm rising, he pushed even deeper into Nadejda and came with a yell.

For a moment, he stayed welded to his partner, making the

pleasure last. It had been a long time since he had felt such a powerful physical sensation.

Finally Nadejda gently pushed him out of her, leaving Malko's sword without a scabbard.

Her eyes lowered, Nadejda picked up her panties, sniffed them, and put them on.

"I'm going to get a glass of orange juice," she said, smiling shyly. And she was gone.

It took Malko some time to come back down to earth. Gocha had given him a poisoned chalice. Nadejda clearly had a terrific career ahead of her.

Emerging from the green salon, Malko saw that the guests were still as numerous as before, drinking and talking loudly. As he reached the bar, someone thumped him on the back.

"She's something else, isn't she?" asked a grinning Gocha.

Feeling a little embarrassed, Malko gave him an ambiguous smile.

"Pretty extraordinary," he admitted.

"If you want to see her again, just tell me. She's gone home to bed. Nadejda leads a very healthy life," Gocha said, quite seriously. "No liquor, no tobacco, lots of sleep."

As Malko poured himself some vodka, Gocha added:

"Irina Lopukin was looking for you earlier. She asked me where you were, but I didn't tell her. I think she's out on the terrace. You're a lucky guy tonight. Irina's a damn good-looking woman."

Leaving Gocha, Malko went out onto the crowded terrace. Some of the couples along the wooden rail were groping each other, but Malko's own libido was switched off. Where Nadejda passed, she left only scorched earth behind.

Suddenly he saw a woman making her way through the crowd toward him: it was Irina, her eyes shining. She took Malko by the arm and led him off to a dark corner.

"Where did you disappear to?" she asked.

"I've been right here."

"No matter. I changed my mind. I would like to see you again."

"Did you *really* change your mind?"

Irina shot him an angry look.

"Yes, I did, and I'll explain why."

"All right. How about dinner tomorrow?"

"No, let's make it the day after. Come to my place; I'll make us a reservation somewhere. I better go now; my friend will be wondering where I am."

She merged into the crowd, leaving Malko feeling puzzled. Why had she done such an about-face? Was it on a sentimental whim, or for some other reason?

He said good-bye to Gocha and walked a few yards along the quay to clear his head. Then he flagged down an old Mercedes and gave the driver four hundred rubles to take him to the Ritz-Carlton.

It was half past noon, and an Audi with tinted windows was waiting in front of the Vysokta. When Irina came out of the building, a bodyguard practically leaped from the car to open the door for her.

Lavrenty Pavlovich had invited her to lunch in one of the Kremlin's private National Security Council dining rooms. This would certainly stymie the FSB agents in charge of her surveillance; they were on hostile territory there. They could follow her only as far as the Kremlin gates. When the black Audi drove through Gate Number 9, they discreetly backed off.

Escorted by a guard, Irina first climbed a monumental staircase, then took an elevator to the second floor, which was a sea of gold and marble. This was one of the most secure areas of the Kremlin, and a man in black stood guard at every hallway corner.

It took them more than five minutes to reach the circular dining room where they would have lunch. Irina was invited to sit on a banquette. She lit a cigarette, in defiance of security regulations.

Now that she was there, though, Irina felt nervous. Was she making a big mistake? she wondered. Once she started the wheels turning, there was no going back.

Irina wasn't doing this to please Malko Linge, but to satisfy her own pride. She couldn't stand being so crudely humiliated by the FSB. She was going to turn their demands around on them.

She almost didn't hear heard Pavlovich enter the room. He was tall and gaunt, almost haggard, and his suit looked too big for him, but his eyes were bright. He came over, took both of Irina's hands, and kissed them tenderly.

"*Dushka!*" he exclaimed. "You're as beautiful as ever! A ray of sunshine for me, since I see only fat, red-faced old apparatchiks all day long."

"You look in pretty good shape yourself."

A shadow passed through Pavlovich's eyes.

"Ah, that's an illusion. I've got something nasty eating at me. But if I lose the fight, I won't let myself be worn down. I'll die like a soldier. Come along, we'll talk a little before having lunch."

They had been lovers more than a decade earlier, but had always retained great affection for each other. She respected him, and he was secretly in love with her.

Pavlovich poured Irina a drink and sat down next to her.

"You're in luck," he said. "I was due to have lunch with the governor of Vladivostok, but he canceled, so I can eat with you. Otherwise you'd have to wait for weeks. So what brings you here today?"

"I just wanted to see you," she said. "Time passes so fast. One of these days, we won't be here anymore."

"That's true," he said, nodding. "But I imagine you must have some other reason, too. Tell me the truth."

Pavlovich was too smart to be fooled, and Irina realized she would have the put her cards on the table. But she wanted to dispel one last worry first.

"Is it safe to talk here?" she asked very quietly.

He smiled.

"As if we were in the middle of a field out in the countryside. Our people do a sweep of all these rooms every morning. And remember, we're the ones who give orders to the *siloviki*. Is what you have to tell me so dangerous?"

"No, but I have some questions. And you don't have to answer, if you don't want to."

"Ask away."

Irina kept her voice low just the same:

"What do you know about the Berezovsky affair?"

Pavlovich seemed surprised.

"You mean his suicide?"

"No, his death."

"I know everything about it," he said calmly. "As do a very few other people. But why are you interested? Did you know him?"

"No, I just want to know what really happened."

He nodded.

"All right, I'll tell you."

CHAPTER

16

Captain Morozov listened impassively as his two agents reported in. Irina Lopukin's visit to the Kremlin was starting to worry him.

"I want to know who she went to see there," he said.

Pavel Bromukin, one of the agents who had followed her, spoke up.

"That's very difficult, sir," he said. "I noted the license number of the car that picked the lady up, but it's from a pool of official vehicles, so the number won't tell us anything.

"I'm not even sure.I'm allowed to enter that *korpus*. You need special authorization, and our ID cards aren't enough. If I start asking questions, I might be taken to security and interrogated. Those people don't fool around, sir. I would have to tell them who sent me."

In other words, this could come back to bite Captain Morozov on the ass. And he didn't know the rank of the person who had invited Irina Lopukin to the Kremlin.

"All right," he said. "The simplest thing will be to ask Gospazha Lopukin herself. Has she contacted this Malko Linge, as we requested?"

"Not to my knowledge," said Bromukin. "She hasn't phoned

him, and they haven't met in person. Last night she went out with one of her men friends, and he brought her home afterward."

"What about Linge himself?"

"He called one of his old friends, a certain Gocha Sukhumi, who invited him to a party at his place in River House."

"Who is this Gocha Sukhumi?"

"He used to be one of ours, sir. He ran the KGB office in Tbilisi until 1990. Then he went into business and made a lot of money. He has known Linge for a long time."

"We should contact him," said the captain.

Bromukin wasn't too enthusiastic.

"He's a pretty tough customer, sir, and he has lots of friends. He won't tell us anything if he doesn't want to, and he can't be pushed. But I'm willing to try anyway."

None of this was looking too good, thought the counterespionage officer. He said:

"If Gospazha Lopukin doesn't contact Linge tomorrow, I'll have her brought in here again. But for now, go stake out Gate Number 9 and watch when she comes out. She might have somebody with her."

Morozov's concern about the Kremlin visit was increasing. He hadn't realized that Irina Lopukin had friends in such high places.

I hope she hasn't gone to complain about me, he thought.

He was a mere captain, and not eager to be shipped out to the provinces somewhere.

Two waiters brought *zakuski* from the Kremlin's Buffet Number 1, and Irina and her host helped themselves to a selection of appetizers. As he finished his herring, Pavlovich asked:

"Do you know about a man called Rem Tolkachev?"

Irina shook her head.

"No. Who is he?"

"One of the most powerful men in the Kremlin. Very few people know him or what he does. I had never heard of him until I joined the council. His office is in the same *korpus* as this one. He's in permanent contact with the president; or I should say 'presidents,' because he has served several of them. Just revealing his name is a federal crime."

"Then why are you telling me about him?" asked a surprised Irina. "I don't want to get you in trouble."

Pavlovich smiled slightly.

"Because you asked me to tell you about the Berezovsky affair, and Tolkachev is the man who organized the whole thing, on President Putin's order. Officially, nothing links him to the case, but I learned about his role from friends in the Moscow FSB."

"Are you sure of this?" asked Irina. "These aren't just rumors, are they?"

"I'm positive. In such a sensitive case, no written records exist. There's a chance that Tolkachev has something in writing, but he would never show it to anyone. However, all sensitive information is shared with us on the Security Council. The most senior FSB officials give us the information in absolute secrecy, so we know what's going on.

"The Berezovsky operation was made easier because it was a 100 percent FSB job. It didn't involve the GRU or any other federal agency. Even within the Service, very few people knew about it. The London *rezidentura* wasn't informed, for example.

"The operation was directed by Tolkachev and carried out by a small group of about a dozen people. They were brought together for this operation only. Afterward, the group disbanded and its members returned to their regular positions."

Irina found herself both fascinated and frightened. She knew how sensitive everything involving the Kremlin was, and Pavlovich's revelations were making her head spin.

"Are you really sure you should be talking to me?" she asked. "You're putting your life in danger, Lavrenty."

He smiled at her sadly.

"My life is already in danger for other reasons, Irina. I don't have long to live. In fact, I'll be stepping down quite soon. This might well be the last favor I can do for you."

"And you aren't betraying your duties?"

He shook his head.

"No, because the Berezovsky affair doesn't affect Russia's security. It was purely personal revenge. He no longer had any political influence, and his death didn't change anything. Except maybe to please President Putin, who got rid of his last enemy, a man who had betrayed him. The president doesn't like traitors. So I'm not revealing any state secrets."

He paused.

"Now, would you like me to tell you how it was actually done? Or at least as much as I can, because I don't know all the details?"

"Of course," said Irina in a hushed voice.

Pavlovich told the story slowly and carefully, pausing from time to time to take a sip of tea and wipe his face. He gave names, dates, and specifics. It was pure gold.

Irina committed it all to memory. She wrote only one thing down, a name and a formula she was afraid she might not remember. When Pavlovich finally fell silent, she realized how exhausted he was. Her friend had bags under his eyes, and his gaze had lost its spark.

He heaved a sigh.

"I don't know if I'll ever see you again, little dove," he said wearily, "but it was a joy to have lunch with you."

Pavlovich stood up first, took Irina's hands in his, and kissed them one after the other.

"I'll have you taken home," he said.

He rang a buzzer and gave an order to the man in black who promptly appeared. He and Irina exchanged a long look, then parted in the hallway. Feeling heartbroken, Irina watched as his slender, slightly hunched figure moved off. She was sure she would never have another friend like him.

Walking behind her guide along the thick blue-and-gold carpeting, Irina wondered what she would do with Pavlovich's revelations. She felt as if she'd been handed a bottle of nitroglycerin that could explode and destroy her along with many other things.

"There she is!"

The FSB team stationed on the other side of Kremlin Gate Number 9 watched as the limousine that carried Irina came out and headed for the Moskva River waterfront. Because of the car's tinted windows, they couldn't tell if the young woman was inside, so they were forced to follow it to the Vysokta building and watch as she got out. The Audi took off again. There was no point in following it; the FSB agents might themselves get arrested.

Her legs weak, Irina let herself fall onto her big mauve sofa. She had often known tantalizing secrets when she was still married to her banker husband, but nothing like what she had just learned.

A little voice told her to forget everything and move on to something else, and she was sorely tempted to follow it.

Just then her cell phone rang, and she started.

She didn't recognize the number but answered anyway. The FSB captain's cold voice sent a chill down her spine.

"Gospazha Lopukin? I hope I'm not disturbing you."

"No. What do you want?"

"We had a deal," the officer said. "You don't seem to be holding up your end of the agreement."

Irina felt a wave of anger. This damned apparatchik was so sure of himself!

"That's where you're wrong, Captain!" she burst out. "I'm having dinner with Malko Linge this evening. He's coming here to get me."

She hung up, furious, but also in some way relieved: the die was cast. Now she just had to decide whether to share Lavrenty Pavlovich's revelations with Malko.

Irina was dressed to kill: a form-hugging embroidered black velvet top, a wide leather Uzbek belt, and an ankle-length skirt with a slit up each side.

"Where are we going?" asked Malko.

"I made a reservation at the Mayak"—a fashionable, expensive restaurant serving international cuisine—she said.

"Great, let's go," he said, and walked out ahead of her.

To avoid the hassle of taxis, Malko had booked one of the Ritz-Carlton's limos: a Mercedes 600 driven by an expressionless young blond man. Malko and Irina hardly said three words during the trip. It was likely that the driver worked for the FSB.

At the Mayak, they were given a table not far from the bar, where a brace of provocative women lay in wait. They had ice-cold eyes and legs that went on and on.

Malko ordered Crimean champagne, *zakuski*, and shoulder of lamb. The mood at the table was strange. Why had Irina agreed to have dinner with him? He waited for the arrival of the lamb before asking the question that was on the tip of his tongue.

"What made you change your mind, Irina?"

She answered that with a question of her own:

"Did you come to Moscow only for the Berezovsky case?"

"That's right. I told you that, but you didn't seem very inclined to help me."

"Things have changed."

"What do you mean?"

"Two things. When we met, I didn't know anything about the case, and that has changed. And some heavy-handed people have tried to restrict my freedom. So I've been trying to decide if I should help you, even if it's dangerous for me."

Malko waited tensely, careful not to break the spell. He could feel the young woman's hesitation.

"I'm listening," he said quietly. "This is an extremely sensitive matter, as you know. It could put you in danger."

"I'm well aware of that," she said tartly. "All right, what do you want to know?"

"Everything," said Malko. "For starters, who was behind the operation, besides Vladimir Putin."

"A man whose name I won't tell you," she said. "An extremely high Kremlin official who regularly handles this kind of problem. He personally assembled a team of very reliable people."

So far, this is nothing to get too excited about, thought Malko.

"Who were the members of the team?" he asked.

"I don't know them all, but one who played a big part is a reporter with *Forbes Russia*."

"Ilya Sokolov?"

"I see I can't tell you anything you don't already know," Irina said with a smile.

"Yes, you can. I know Sokolov played a role in the operation, but I don't know if it was significant."

"His role was essential," said Irina. "In fact, he had several roles.

First, he was assigned to latch on to Berezovsky so the killers could track him. And he contributed to the disinformation program afterward, claiming that Berezovsky had told him he was tired of living. But most of all, Sokolov was the man who brought the poison to England."

"What poison?"

"Boris Berezovsky was killed with a very rare poison that doesn't leave any traces in the body and makes the death look like a heart attack. It's manufactured here in Russia. Sokolov carried it to England and gave it to the killers."

"Can you describe it?"

Irina took out a piece of paper from her purse, and set it on the table.

"This is what it's called."

Malko picked up the note: *sodium fluoride*, followed by a chemical formula.

"A dose of 2.5 to 10 grams is lethal," she said. "It acts from between a few minutes and up to twelve hours, which gave the killers time to 'prepare' Berezovsky in staging his phony suicide. He was already dead when they brought him into the bathroom to set it up."

Irina put the paper back in her purse after Malko finished copying the formula into his notepad.

Malko felt as if he was making progress, even though he didn't have any tangible evidence yet.

"So Sokolov works with the FSB?" he asked.

"Of course! A lot of journalists do, but he has a special status. He doesn't just work for them from time to time."

"Is he here in Moscow?"

"I imagine so, but there's no point trying to see him. The moment the FSB finds out, they will know that you know, and that will be very dangerous for both of us."

"Do you know anything about the members of the kill team?"

"No."

In the silence that followed, Malko scanned the dining room and spotted two men at a table above theirs, looking at them.

"We're being watched," he said quietly. "I hope those men didn't notice that piece of paper."

"Whatever! Is there anything else you want to know?"

"Yes. Why was Boris Berezovsky killed now?"

Irina smiled.

"That's probably the most interesting piece of information I was told. The Berezovsky affair wraps up a long dispute between Britain and Russia. David Cameron, the new prime minister, made a deal with Putin. In exchange for some commercial agreements, Britain agreed to close the Litvinenko case, which was still open.

"The British foreign secretary ordered the judge in the case not to reveal classified evidence that was compromising to Russia, in the name of national security. Sir Robert Owen, the coroner, obeyed reluctantly. But there was still some danger: the case was about to be revived, and Berezovsky was due to testify.

"He could've made some very embarrassing revelations. So it was important that he be eliminated before the case was reopened."

Malko was astonished.

What Irina was saying suggested high-level complicity between the British and the Russians. It wasn't a murder anymore, but an affair of state.

"So, do you know enough?" she asked. "I've told you everything I know. I think we can go home now."

Without taking his eyes off the couple's table, one of the FSB agents whispered to his partner:

"Did you see the paper she showed him?"

"Yes," said Bromukin. "I don't know what it is, but we have to get it."

"That's easy," the other agent said. "We'll just take her in for questioning."

Bromukin frowned. He knew the young woman had influential friends. Better to act more subtly. Besides, they couldn't be sure the piece of paper had any connection to their mission.

"Let's follow them and ask headquarters for orders," he suggested. "The American agent wrote something down. Let's pursue that first. It'll be easier to put the squeeze on him."

CHAPTER

17

When the limo stopped in front of the Vysokta, Irina Lopukin turned to Malko and said:

"So, there you have it. I hope I've been of some help."

"You've been incredibly helpful," he said. "But I don't want us to say good-bye like this. Can I come up for a drink?"

After the briefest of hesitations, the young woman nodded and got out of the Mercedes. Malko followed, leaving the driver to find a parking place and wait.

In the apartment, Irina tossed her purse onto the coffee table and walked over to the bar. She came back with two glasses and a bottle of Tsarskaya vodka, and they drank a toast.

Glancing at Irina's purse, Malko said:

"You know the piece of paper you showed me earlier? The people watching us saw it, so you should destroy it. Unless you need it, that is."

"No, I don't."

She took out the paper and burned it in the ashtray with her lighter. It was gone in a few seconds, and Malko felt better. From now on, he would be the one taking the risks.

Irina poured herself a second vodka and downed it. Then, in a perfectly natural movement, she let her head rest on Malko's shoulder. It was the first intimate gesture she had allowed herself since their initial encounter. Turning her head, her lips brushed Malko's, then parted in a passionate kiss.

Within moments, he was rediscovering the curves of a body he had briefly explored seven years earlier. When he touched Irina's full breasts, she stirred and drove her tongue deeper into his mouth. He almost felt she was going to devour his lips.

Then she pulled off her velvet top, keeping on only a black bra. Without removing her skirt, she stretched out on the long mauve sofa and laid her head on a pillow. When she raised one leg, the skirt's long slit parted, exposing her thigh.

Malko's hand moved slowly up her leg to the top of a stay-up stocking. Encountering a black string panty a little farther up, he snagged it with his fingers and slid it down.

Irina submitted, her eyes closed in an almost dreamlike trance. Then she gradually began to move, arching her back under his caresses, breathing faster.

She unhooked her bra, freeing her breasts.

"Lick my tits," she said hoarsely. "I love that."

The vodka had done its work.

When his lips touched one strawberry-like nipple, it immediately stiffened under his tongue. Irina had gone directly from coldness to passion.

Her hips rose higher and higher. Then she pushed Malko's fingers away and instead, in an unmistakable gesture, pulled his head down to her crotch.

When Malko put his mouth on her, Irina heaved a long, easy sigh. It became a spasm and a cry of pleasure when his tongue reached her clit. Thighs spread wide, she held Malko's head in both hands, against the unlikely possibility that he would pull away from her.

Suddenly she gave a scream of joy and fell back stunned, as waves of pleasure rolled over her.

While Malko was catching his breath, his cock, which was as stiff as a poker, now had just one goal: Irina's cunt. But before it could put its plan into effect, the young woman took it in her mouth as hungrily as a starving predator. Sucking Malko's cock with the fervor of a vestal virgin, Irina brought him to orgasm, and he collapsed on the sofa, spent.

After a long moment, Irina slowly slipped on her panties and hooked her bra.

"You really made me come," she said with a pleasant yawn. "I'm happy to have seen you again, even if it was thanks to those FSB morons. When are you leaving town?"

"I'm not sure. I don't think I'll be staying much longer."

In fact, Malko was now eager to get back to London with the invaluable information Irina had given him. He looked at the little pile of ashes in the ashtray and touched a tiny scrap of paper.

Irina led him to the front door and offered him her lips with a somewhat vague smile.

"Watch out for yourself!"

She stumbled off to her bedroom, her legs wobbly, and let herself fall onto her bed. The next time she saw the FSB people, she would have something to tell them.

Malko was crossing the Ritz-Carlton lobby when two men appeared beside him. *Siloviki*, from the looks of them.

One flashed an ID card with a tricolor stripe and politely said:

"Gospodin Linge, we have instructions to take you to Bolshaya Lubyanka."

Malko stiffened.

"Why?"

"Just a routine check, sir. It won't take long."

It was never long with the FSB, just a century or two. But what was the point of resisting? The notepad where Malko had written the poison and its formula was in his pocket, but it was too late to get rid of it.

"Very well," he said. "I'll just phone my embassy."

One of the officers shook his head.

"Don't bother, gospodin. This will take an hour at most. Come with us, please."

They led him outside to a black Audi. Light bar flashing, the car drove silently down Tverskaya Ulitsa, then turned left toward Lubyanka Square. Nothing was said until they reached FSB headquarters. As polite as ever, the two agents took Malko up to the third floor in an elevator and ushered him into an office with neon lights.

"Empty your pockets," said one indifferently.

Malko did so. They put his things into a plastic bag and went out, leaving him alone.

He heard a key turn in the door, locking him in.

Malko's effects had been spread out on a table, and FSB agents were carefully photographing them under the direction of the duty sergeant. Malko's notepad got special treatment. A number of close-ups were taken of a line of writing a few words long: *sodium fluoride, 2.5–10 mg*, followed by a formula. When they were finished, the agents put everything in a clear plastic envelope, and the sergeant went to another office to screen the photographs.

Noticing the mysterious phrase, he immediately called the captain who was coordinating the Linge surveillance. An hour had already passed since Malko's arrest.

"What should we do with the suspect, sir?" asked the sergeant. "Take him down to the Lubyanka?"

It wasn't a decision the captain couldn't make on his own

authority. It was already past midnight, and his superiors were sound asleep.

"Bring him some tea," he ordered. "He can lie down if he likes."

Meanwhile, the captain had to find someone in charge to decide Malko's fate. At this hour, it wasn't clear who that would be. It took another hour before he got a sleepy superior to order him to release the suspect.

Malko had already drunk two cups of tea when the agents who had detained him at the Ritz-Carlton reappeared, carrying his affairs.

"Sorry to make you wait," one of them said blandly. "We had to check a few things, and that took time. Everything is in order. We'll bring you back to your hotel now."

Not a word about why he'd been arrested.

Malko took his possessions without looking at them. The FSB had its faults, but they weren't thieves. The inevitable black Audi was waiting in the courtyard, and ten minutes later he was back at the Ritz-Carlton.

The moment he got to his room, Malko went through all his things and checked his notepad. Everything was there, but the Russians had surely noted the name of the poison Irina gave him.

First thing in the morning, he would go to the CIA station, which would assign him bodyguards. Then he had to get out of Russia as soon as possible—if he could.

He had trouble falling asleep.

As he did every morning, Rem Tolkachev reached his office at eight. He had bought himself a strong cup of tea while waiting for the daily delivery of documents from the FSB. They arrived twenty minutes later. On top of the stack, he noticed a thick file stamped "Secret" and immediately started reading it.

An FSB captain reported that while following the CIA agent Malko Linge, the subject had been seen writing down some words communicated to him by Irina Lopukin. In an effort of efficiency, he had the agent detained and brought to Service headquarters. This had resulted in the discovery of some writing whose meaning he did not know.

Tolkachev peered at a close-up photo that showed the details of the text in question.

And nearly had a heart attack.

The spymaster was looking at one of Russia's most closely held secrets! The text was no mystery to him. He had personally ordered the poison from one of the secret laboratories that worked for the FSB, and the substance had moved through his office to England, where it ended Boris Berezovsky's life.

Baffled, Tolkachev examined the words written on the notepad. How could Malko Linge have come into possession of the secret, which was known to only a handful of people?

It no longer had any practical importance, since Berezovsky was dead and buried, and even an autopsy wouldn't reveal anything. So there were no immediate consequences, except that now somebody knew. It couldn't be Irina Lopukin. So who had told her the secret?

Tolkachev was boiling with impotent rage. He couldn't let such an affront go unpunished.

Even if the damage was already done, the two people who were in the know had to die.

Irina Lopukin was one thing, but Malko Linge was more complicated. Tolkachev had plenty of ways to hit him without it looking like murder, but that might make waves. He decided to take his time.

He sat down and typed a highly confidential note to the head of FSB special operations.

"Your life is in grave danger," said the Moscow CIA station chief, on hearing Malko describe the previous night's events.

"You're in possession of top secret information, and they'll do everything they can to kill you," he said. "I'm immediately assigning you some special ops 'babysitters.' That's better than nothing, but you have to get out of Moscow as soon as possible. And not on a Russian plane. I'll put you on the next British Airways flight."

Garden asked his secretary to book a single ticket for London. When she came back a few minutes later, she looked apologetic.

"The BA flight is full," she said. "I tried two others; same thing. Yet this isn't the busy travel season."

Malko smiled sourly.

"It's their usual procedure. Keep me from flying out while they plan what to do next. Of course, I could always catch a train."

"I'll ask Langley for instructions," said the station chief. "In the meantime you're not leaving the embassy; they won't come after you here. And let's have lunch together."

Tolkachev was fuming. The Berezovsky operation had gone off without a hitch, yet now there was a fly in the ointment. The image of the Kremlin he was sworn to protect was at risk.

A quick investigation revealed how the information could have leaked. Irina Lopukin had paid a visit to Lavrenty Pavlovich, the vice chair of the National Security Council. He would know about the poison, but why would he tell Lopukin? There was no way to ask him directly. Pavlovich was seriously ill and had just been hospitalized. Given his rank, he could hardly be dragged down to FSB headquarters for questioning.

Tolkachev decided he would deal with that problem later. For now, he had to settle the fate of the two people who had learned the secret, even if it had no immediate impact on Berezovsky's killing.

Having the name of the poison was only dangerous in connection with certain other information that Linge had no way of knowing. Still, Tolkachev wanted to wrap up the case for the president, and that meant eliminating two people who knew something they shouldn't.

He typed a note for the head of the FSB, giving him precise instructions.

Sitting in an office reserved for visiting CIA operatives, Malko felt grumpy and restless. After a bite at the embassy snack bar, he'd communicated with Langley and the London station, giving them the name of the poison used to kill Berezovsky. Langley's answer arrived an hour later. The substance was known to have been used in other killings. It was made in a certain secret Russian laboratory; the CIA knew its location.

Unfortunately, that information didn't advance Malko's investigation right now.

His trip to Moscow was turning out to be only marginally more successful than the one to Israel. He now knew more about the arrangements of the killing and the role of the *Forbes Russia* journalist, but only enough to flesh out a report, not lead him to the killers.

The answer he sought was still in London, he knew. He had to find the person Sokolov had given the poison to, and the journalist himself certainly wouldn't tell him.

But to return to London, Malko had to get out of the country, and the Russians were up to their usual tricks to keep him here.

It would give them time to figure out a way to attack him between the time he left the embassy and was safely aboard a British Airways plane. FSB agents were endlessly creative, and they had sophisticated technical means at their disposal. They might try poison, a car accident, a mugging gone wrong—anything.

Malko felt he was living on borrowed time. Even surrounded by a squad of special ops men, his life would be in danger the moment he stepped outside the embassy.

As he leafed through the day's *New York Times*, he reflected that Gwyneth Robertson was now the key to his investigation. She was the only person who could lead him to the man who had organized Berezovsky's phony suicide and had tried to kill Malko himself.

Arkady Lianin.

If he was still in London, that is.

Roy Garden opened the door, a serious expression on his face.

"I've just been told that two FSB cars are parked across from the embassy. I'm sure they're for you."

The trap was beginning to close.

"We just have to wait," Malko said with a shrug. "When a seat on my flight suddenly becomes available, then we'll know they're ready to kill me."

CHAPTER

18

It was two o'clock in the morning, and traffic along the banks of the Moskva had eased considerably. Igor Stelin heard a car stop out front, but the Vysokta night porter didn't bother looking up from his newspaper. There weren't any visitors at this late hour, and he paid no attention to the regular tenants.

But when the front door swung open and three men came in, he immediately knew that they weren't any of the building's normal visitors.

The three were practically clones. They were young, with smooth, determined faces that looked a bit vacant. They wore gray suits and carried leather briefcases. They headed straight for the elevators without a glance at the old man at the front desk—as if they knew their way around the building perfectly.

Normally, Stelin would have asked them whom they had come to see, but he was paralyzed. These people were different, and as a good Russian, he could sense it.

They were *siloviki*.

Their ease, self-confidence, and indifference all spoke volumes.

Stelin felt as if he were nailed to the spot. In Russia, an ordinary citizen who got in a *silovik*'s way could pay a very high price, crushed by a blind, all-powerful administrative machine acting on orders from above.

Still, his sense of duty caused Stelin to stand up. He didn't have time to do more. Before disappearing down the hallway, the third man in gray turned around and stared at him.

Even at that distance, the look in his eyes was clear: Igor Stelin had not seen them, and would never say he had. They were phantoms, protected by the law.

It only lasted a fraction of a second, then the man vanished.

Stelin slumped back onto his chair, defeated.

The three men stopped at the door to Irina Lopukin's apartment. The hallway was deserted. From his briefcase, one took a set of lock picks and a stethoscope. A specialist, he had worked for years in the FSB department, charged with breaking into foreign embassies. No lock could resist him, and when he opened one, he left such minute scratches, they could only be seen with a microscope.

Irina's deadbolt took him less than two minutes.

After a few clicks, the bolt slid back. The men pushed the door open and slipped into the apartment, closing the door behind them. One took out a floor plan. Lighting it with a tiny flashlight, he led the others to Irina's bedroom. The team walked in single file. The flashlight kept them from bumping into the furniture.

They stopped at the bedroom door, which was ajar, and listened carefully. They heard nothing. Irina must have been asleep. FSB surveillance had shown that she was home, but she might have been reading or watching television.

The team leader took a pre-loaded syringe from his kit. It had a 3 mm needle so fine that an injection left no trace. He checked the syringe's contents, then put on a pair of night-vision goggles so he could make out people and objects in the dark.

He nodded to the others to signify that he was ready, and pushed the door open. The bedroom lay in darkness, but he could see Irina sleeping on her side in the big bed. He walked over slowly, followed by one of his teammates. They observed her for a few moments, listening to her regular breathing. She hadn't stirred at their entrance.

This was the most delicate moment of the operation.

The team leader leaned over the sleeping woman, who was wearing a nightgown and was covered by a sheet. Her neck was the only exposed part of her body. He gently slid the syringe's needle into the skin above her collarbone, and pressed the plunger, injecting a powerful anesthetic.

The sting was so slight that Irina barely reacted, just brushed the injection site with her hand, as if to chase a mosquito away. The man had already withdrawn the syringe, so her hand met only empty air.

He straightened up, breathing hard. His partner had stepped around the bed, ready to pinion her in case she awoke.

She didn't.

Irina looked as if she were simply sleeping. But without being aware of it, she was moving from natural sleep into an anesthesia that would last about half an hour.

The leader waited a few minutes, then switched on the bedside light and got rid of his night-vision goggles.

The others pulled the sheet off the sleeping woman and stretched her out, spreading her feet.

The leader took another pre-loaded syringe from his kit and slipped on a head lamp with a reflector to help him see clearly.

He massaged Irina's right foot for a moment, then pressed on a vein to raise it. Deftly stabbing the vein with the second syringe, he quickly injected its contents. When he pulled the needle out, it didn't even leave a drop of blood.

To be on the safe side, he rubbed the vein for a moment to make the nearly invisible puncture disappear completely. Then he covered Irina with the sheet again. They turned off the bedside lamp and left the bedroom.

To all appearances, she was sound asleep.

The anesthesia would wear off in a few minutes, but before it did, the 10 mg of deadly sodium fluoride would be silently circulating in her bloodstream.

She would never wake up. Before daybreak, the poison she'd been given would stop her heart. A doctor examining her could only conclude that she died of a heart attack. An autopsy would reveal nothing out of the ordinary.

The Lopukin problem had been taken care of.

.

When the men in gray passed by the night porter again, he went on reading his paper, keeping his eyes downcast. The three filed out into the darkness, heading for a black car parked a little distance away.

Stelin tried to concentrate on what he was reading. He was struggling to convince himself that he hadn't seen anybody.

Malko awoke very early—ten past six—because the curtains in his embassy bedroom let in the springtime sun. It was going to be a beautiful day. He had slept badly, tossing and turning as he mulled over the pieces of information he was collecting.

Berezovsky's murder was a textbook illustration of the cunning the Kremlin used in eliminating its enemies. No shots had been fired, no obvious violence used. Just a quick, invisible strike that left no clues.

How much did the British know about this? Malko wondered.

He found it hard to believe that MI5, with all its intelligence-gathering assets, was completely in the dark. British agents weren't fools. Even if they were ordered to keep their mouths shut, they knew. That might be the most frightening aspect of the whole affair. Russia's totalitarian regime was corrupting a true democracy, making it the passive accomplice to a state crime.

Malko took a shower and went down to the cafeteria. He was finishing his breakfast when the CIA station chief appeared.

"I was looking for you in your room," Garden said. "I have news."

"What's up?"

"You have a seat on the British Airways noon flight."

So the Russians were letting him leave Moscow! Or else they had prepared a sophisticated way to kill him on the way to the airport.

"What's our setup?"

"We'll drive to Sheremetyevo in two armored cars. I'll come along in one, and we'll have bodyguards in the other. I can accompany you as far as the customs gate. They won't allow me to go beyond that."

"Let's keep our fingers crossed," said Malko. "I don't want to spend the rest of my life here in the embassy."

"Okay," said Garden. "We're leaving at ten."

Rem Tolkachev took the document with the red wax seal from the stack of freshly delivered papers. An envelope bearing the Moscow FSB logo, it contained a very brief account of the night operation he had ordered. It had gone off without a hitch. The Lopukin problem had been solved, permanently.

It would be just one of the many poisonings that marked the history of Russia and the Soviet Union. None of the killers were ever arrested, of course; though a few innocent people chose to plead guilty. If you torture someone enough, they'll confess to anything.

Assuming everything else went well today, Tolkachev would finally be able to close the Berezovsky file and report to the president that his orders had been carried out.

It was now time for the second part of his plan.

Tolkachev phoned the head of FSB special operations on an encrypted line to check on his preparations.

"The arrangements are all in place, sir," the officer assured him. "We have six vehicles, counting the two across from the embassy. Everything will go off as planned."

"I hope so," said the spymaster coldly. "As you are aware, this involves the elimination of an enemy of the *rodina*, to which the highest authorities attach enormous importance."

Which meant that if the operation failed, the person in charge would be subject to sanctions that would end his career. Or his life.

Two armored Mercedes with diplomatic plates awaited in the embassy courtyard, their drivers ready. When Malko and Garden came down, four bodyguards were in the escort vehicle.

As the CIA station chief was heading for the lead Mercedes, Malko called out to him.

"Roy, I have an idea. Let's you and I get into the second car. We can move two officers into the first one."

"Why?"

"I'm not sure, and it probably isn't necessary," said Malko, "but it doesn't cost anything. If one of the vehicles is targeted, it'll be the first one."

The Russians might very well have snipers along the highway to the airport. Malko remembered that Afghan president Karzai had recently avoided being killed because he wasn't in the car that a would-be assassin had shot at. Garden agreed, and ordered two of the bodyguards into the first Mercedes while he and Malko took their places in the second. The passengers couldn't be seen through the tinted windows, so the Russians wouldn't be aware of the switch.

Once everyone was seated, the metal gate slid open and the two vans emerged from the courtyard and took Bolshoy Deviatsky Pereulok, driving fast. Within twenty minutes, they were passing Belorussky Station on their way to Leningradsky Prospekt, the broad highway leading to Sheremetyevo Airport.

At that point, they had just a dozen miles to go.

Malko was scanning the highway, but he didn't see anything suspicious. The green lights on Leningradsky Prospekt were very long, so as not to slow traffic.

A mile farther on, the light ahead turned green. That was perfectly normal, but Malko immediately noticed something strange. Instead of turning red, the light on the cross street stayed yellow, which would let cars coming from the right pull into the main flow of traffic. Fortunately, there was no traffic on the cross street.

That sort of thing happened often enough in Moscow, and Malko went back to watching the road. They were now just a few hundred yards from the intersection.

Suddenly, he was horrified to see a huge Ural truck roaring down the cross street toward them. Traveling at high speed, it would reach the intersection at the exact same moment as the embassy vehicles.

CHAPTER

19

With his eyes fixed on Leningradsky Prospekt, the CIA station chief hadn't noticed anything amiss.

"Roy!" yelled Malko.

Their little convoy's lead Mercedes had just entered the intersection, and its driver either didn't see the truck or assumed it would yield the right of way. Instead, it roared into the crossing on a collision course with the car.

In a terrible shock, the truck's huge bumper plowed into the Mercedes's right rear door. The car rolled over twice and wound up on its roof, as other cars swerved wildly to get out of the way.

It all happened in seconds.

As Malko's car entered the intersection, the Ural continued straight ahead, barreling across Leningradsky Prospekt without hitting any other vehicles, and roared away on a crossroad. Malko and Roy Garden watched in horror as the car they should have been riding in burst into flames.

The CIA station chief screamed at his driver:

"Stop the car!"

"No, don't!" yelled Malko. "We've got to keep going!"

In any case, they were caught in the flow of traffic, with cars in front and behind, so the driver continued. A column of black smoke rose behind them, but was soon lost to sight. Deathly pale,

Garden tried to call the driver of the burning Mercedes on the phone.

In vain.

"Alert the embassy!" said Malko. "There's nothing we can do."

He was shaken. If he hadn't had the idea of changing to the second car, he would have been burned alive.

Garden was talking breathlessly into his phone, telling the embassy what had happened. His hands were shaking.

"My God, they're all dead," he mumbled.

"Maybe not," said Malko, though he didn't really believe that the driver and the two case officers could have survived.

Traffic eased, and the Mercedes was able to speed up.

The station chief seemed stunned.

"Do you still want to leave?" he managed to say.

"I don't have any choice," said Malko. "I doubt they've set anything up at the airport to intercept me, since I wasn't supposed to ever get there. This is an FSB operation. The border guards probably don't know anything about it."

"We've lost three men, and we'll never be able to avenge them," said Garden dully. "The Russians won't find the truck, and it'll be blamed on a reckless driver."

His phone rang. It was the embassy, which had sent a convoy to the scene of the accident.

They passed a sign: *Sheremetyevo 4 km.*

A man in a *militciya* uniform was sitting on his patrol motorcycle next to the unit that controlled the intersection stoplight. He got off, walked over to the controller cabinet and opened it with a special key.

Flipping a switch restored the red-yellow-green pattern he had changed to steady yellow a few minutes earlier. He closed the box and climbed back on his motorcycle.

The signal was working normally again. If there was an investigation, it would conclude that the Ural driver had run a red light. The *militciya* officer, who was actually an FSB agent, headed downtown.

A *militciya* patrol car, parked some distance up the road to prevent cars other than the truck from crossing on the yellow light, quietly drove away.

Aside from the Mercedes burning in the middle of Leningradsky Prospekt, now surrounded by fire trucks and ambulances, no evidence of the operation remained.

The Ural truck, which didn't have any license plates, was on its way to a secret FSB garage. It would never be found.

Malko walked into the Sheremetyevo terminal with his stomach in knots, accompanied by an ashen-faced Roy Garden. The two men headed for the business class check-in counter. There were few people in line, and Malko got his boarding pass within minutes. Like a robot, he walked toward immigration.

Garden's phone rang. After listening for a moment, he said:

"It's terrible; they're all dead. My deputy is on-site."

The two men faced each other. This was as far as the station chief could go.

"I hope you make it to London safely," he said.

"So do I," said Malko soberly.

Malko knew how anxious Garden was to return to the accident scene, so he shook his hand and let him go.

Turning, he handed his passport to a blue-uniformed immigration officer, who ran it through a scanner, then examined and stamped it. He returned it to Malko without comment.

To him, the Austrian with the golden eyes was just another traveler.

Malko walked to the transit lounge and sank into a large armchair. His mind was racing, and he had trouble keeping his hands from shaking. A vision of the huge truck smashing into the Mercedes kept rising to his mind.

A glance at his watch showed forty minutes until his departure time. Forty minutes of fear.

The Russians could still try to keep him from leaving the country.

One of the phones on Rem Tolkachev's desk was blinking: his direct line to the FSB.

"Gospodin Tolkachev?" asked the caller in a neutral voice.

"Yes."

"I want to report that the operation was carried out successfully. The car and its occupants are totally incinerated. The bodies are burned beyond recognition, at least at this point. A detachment from the American embassy is at the scene, and we are treating them with every courtesy. Traffic will be completely restored in an hour."

Tolkachev didn't give a damn about the traffic, but he thanked the man anyway. Then, because he was conscientious, he added:

"Connect me with the border guards at Sheremetyevo."

Each time a newcomer wandered into the departure area, Malko jumped. To distract himself, he ordered a cup of coffee. It tasted like dishwater.

Suddenly two men without any luggage walked in, and Malko's pulse sped up, but they strolled around and left without speaking to anyone. He looked at the clock: twenty more minutes. To give himself something to do, he went to the bathroom. That took five minutes.

The closer it got to departure time, the tenser he became.

He felt he'd lost all sense of time when a loudspeaker announced the boarding of British Airways flight 443. With an effort, he kept from leaping to his feet, then mingled with the few other passengers heading for the gate. He felt as if everyone was watching him. A few moments later, he handed his boarding pass to a ticket agent, who waved him on.

He expected to see police officers appear at any second. Here, the Russians were on home ground; they could do whatever they wanted. Like an automaton, he marched down the Jetway and onto the Boeing 777.

He showed his boarding pass to a flight attendant and sat down. He immediately fastened his seat belt, as if it would somehow protect him.

He counted the passengers entering the plane. Finally he heard the magic phrase "Boarding is now complete." The plane door was closed, and a flight attendant started to recite the safety precautions.

The big Boeing began to move, heading out to the runway.

Malko knew that he wasn't in the clear yet. The control tower could still make the plane return to the gate.

Clutching his armrests, he stared out at the runway, his mouth dry and the sight of the flaming Mercedes before his eyes. After what seemed like an eternity, the plane began to roll and he wanted to shout for joy. Sunk in his seat, he watched the grass along the runway blur by. Finally, the 777's wheels left the ground, and it rose above the great forest around Sheremetyevo and through the cloud cover above it. Malko closed his eyes, his heart still pounding.

With every passing minute he felt danger falling away, but as long as he was in Russian airspace, he was still at risk. The people pursuing him were powerful enough to make a passenger plane turn around and come back. He'd already seen that they would stop at nothing.

He had escaped from Moscow, but at what price?

Rem Tolkachev was in a fever of impatience. More than forty minutes had passed since he'd asked for the border guards at Sheremetyevo. He had phoned three times without getting through.

Finally, his phone blinked, and a deferential border guard colonel came on the line.

"What information would you like, sir?"

"The list of passengers who have checked in for British Airways flight 443."

"I will have to call you back, sir. Our computer system and inside phone lines are all down."

"All right, fine! Just check one name. Has an Austrian citizen named Malko Linge checked in?"

"I'll get back to you, sir."

The spymaster had to wait another ten minutes before his phone blinked again. The same deferential officer said:

"A Mr. Malko Linge has gone through immigration, sir."

"Good God!" muttered Tolkachev through clenched teeth. The man who supposedly burned to death on Leningradsky Prospekt was slipping through his fingers.

"Find him and take him into custody!" he screamed, beside himself with rage. "Linge is wanted by the Moscow FSB. He's got to be in a departure area somewhere. Whatever you do, he mustn't board that flight!"

"Very well, sir," said the colonel. "I'll take care of that right away and call you back."

Tolkachev again found himself staring at a silent telephone. To pass the time, he lit one of his pastel cigarettes, taking slow, deliberate puffs to calm his nerves.

When the phone blinked again, he lunged for it.

"Did you find him?"

"Yes, sir, but unfortunately he'd already boarded the British Airways flight."

"Stop the plane from leaving!"

"That's impossible, sir. It took off ten minutes ago."

The old spymaster nearly choked with rage.

"Colonel, send me a message with your name and rank," he snapped. "I'm holding you personally responsible for this failure."

Malko gazed at his lunch tray. He wasn't hungry; too many emotions. The plane was now at thirty-six thousand feet, heading west.

His brain had started working again.

The final stage of his journey was London, where everything would be dependent on Gwyneth Robertson. Had she managed to find Arkady Lianin's trail?

CHAPTER

20

"What happened in Moscow confirms that the Berezovsky affair is of crucial importance in the Russians' eyes," said Stanley Dexter, leaning back in his office chair. "They would never risk killing members of the embassy unless they had an order directly from the Kremlin."

"Well, we knew this was an affair of state," said Malko. "And we figured out the mechanism, thanks to you. But that's not enough. With the information I've gathered, I could send a first-class report to Langley, and it would just gather dust in a safe somewhere. We need to make headway, and the only way to do that is to find Arkady Lianin, if he's still in England."

"What then?" asked the CIA station chief.

"Offer him a deal. For the Russians, he's now a security risk, and they'll try to kill him or bring him back to Moscow. We have to beat them to the punch. Which means contacting him somehow."

"Can you think of a way to do that?"

"It will depend on Gwyneth Robertson. Either she hasn't made any progress, and we're dead in the water, or she's managed to learn where Lianin is hiding. I'll find out this evening. We have a dinner date."

"Good luck," said Dexter. "It may be our last hope. I'm going to assign you some bodyguards just in case. After what happened in

Moscow . . . The Russians have a very long reach. Where are you meeting?"

"At the Lanesborough."

"Fine. I'll assign you four case officers, in two teams."

He paused.

"Aren't you afraid of putting Miss Robertson in danger?"

"Yes, but I don't have any choice."

At the Lanesborough, the Library Bar was thronged with the usual crowd: up-market prostitutes of every stripe, Russians passing through London, and a variety of fauna of indeterminate provenance.

Malko sipped his ice-cold vodka. Gwyneth was late. That wasn't a good sign, since she was normally very punctual. Dexter's warning came to mind. The Russians could still pull some dirty trick to end Malko's investigation permanently.

Just then, Gwyneth made a striking entrance. She strode into the bar wearing a Chanel suit with a very short skirt, a jacket open over a moiré blouse, and that horny-slut look that drew all eyes wherever she went.

The unattached males in the bar snapped to attention as she passed, but she made her way to Malko's table and sat down in a cloud of perfume.

"Did you have a good trip?" she asked, crossing her legs in their smoky-gray stockings and giving Malko a mischievous glance.

"Not exactly," he said. "Would you like something to drink?"

"Champagne. Roederer, if possible."

Malko ordered, and they toasted each other. Gwyneth looked sexy as hell, and the Library gawkers had no way of knowing who she really was.

Malko noticed when a pair of CIA bodyguards casually went to sit at the end of the bar. Their jackets hid the holsters, so it wasn't obvious that they were armed. Gwyneth spotted them too.

"Do you think we're in any danger?" she asked. "This is one of the most elegant places in London!"

"Yes, and it's full of Russians. I've seen what those people are capable of."

With that, he launched into the tale of his Moscow misadventures. At the third glass of champagne, Gwyneth stopped him.

"What you're saying doesn't surprise me. It's a Kremlin plot, with unlimited means. You're a monkey wrench in the operation, so they'd love to get rid of you."

Malko was dying to ask if she had learned anything, but he held his tongue. As if to tease him, she stretched languorously and announced:

"I'm hungry! Let's get a bite to eat at the Dorchester. Their sole is delicious."

It was just on the other side of Hyde Park Corner.

"Do you have your car?" he asked.

"Of course."

Malko signed the check, and they went outside, where a valet swathed in gold braid handed Gwyneth the key to her Bentley. Malko felt a small surge of pleasure as he slipped into the rich, aromatic leather seat. Luxury was nice.

Gwyneth's skirt hiked up when she slid behind the wheel, baring part of her thighs.

"You're as beautiful as ever," he said.

"Is that why you're taking me to dinner?" she asked impishly.

"It would be reason enough."

It took them only ten minutes to reach the Dorchester, where Gwyneth parked next to a bright yellow Lamborghini before walking into the old hotel.

———

"I was right, the sole is yummy," she said, tearing into a fish the size of a small shark.

Malko had ordered a meltingly tender slice of roast beef swimming in its juices. For a moment, they ate in silence.

Finally, Gwyneth pushed her plate away and looked up at Malko.

"Considering what I've been doing, I really must be fond of you," she said with a sigh.

"Is it as bad as all that?" he asked, suddenly feeling awkward.

She frowned.

"I usually have sex with whoever I like. But this is different. Here's a man who's crazy in love with me, and I have to play a part. Even if it's enjoyable, it's not the same thing."

She took a puff on an electronic cigarette.

"Have you learned anything, at least?" he asked, struggling to sound casual, while hanging on her every word.

The young American let the suspense last for a moment, then reached into her purse.

"I think so!" she exclaimed, handing Malko a folded sheet of paper.

It was a letter written on the stationery of Winstanley-Burgess, Solicitors, and addressed to Constable Harold Bursley, Community Protection Unit, Plaistow Police Station. The letter's subject was the Tourias.

It stated that the British Home Office had granted political asylum to Mr. Touria and his family, per reference C 502360. It went on to note that Mr. Touria was indeed the person he claimed to be. Moreover, he was not considered a threat to Great Britain, and he was of no particular interest to the intelligence services. It continued:

We have recently learned that Mr. Touria is the subject of an $800,000 assassination contract taken out by a criminal orga-

nization in Eastern Europe whose members can enter Great Britain freely.

In consequence, certain precautions have been taken, and Mr. Touria's two children attend school under a different name, for their protection.

We also draw your attention to the fact that Mr. Touria's life may be in danger as a result of this threat.

A surprised Malko put the letter down.

"Who is this Touria person?"

Gwyneth gave him a guileless smile.

"Can't you guess?"

"You don't mean Arkady Lianin!"

"Yup!"

Malko could hardly believe it. The man who had tried to kill him—and who had probably set up the Berezovsky assassination—was under the jurisdiction of the British Home Office and allowed to live in England under a phony name and police protection!

It was incredible.

Gwyneth looked at him, smiling.

"It came as a shock to me too," she admitted.

"Are you sure it's Lianin?"

"Absolutely. James has seen another document that connects the two names and even gives an address, 111 Newham Way. Without naming the town, unfortunately."

"So why is Lianin getting this special treatment?"

"No idea. I imagine he did some favors for MI5. It always works that way. They must've debriefed him, then set him up in some quiet place out in the burbs."

"Do you think the English are aware of his involvement in the Berezovsky business?"

"Hard to tell," she said with a frown. "I also don't know if MI5 is providing him round-the-clock protection. But I'd be surprised if they didn't have their suspicions about what happened."

A hush descended on them, flying the Russian flag and the Union Jack together.

The affair was becoming more and more complicated.

"Can you find out where he's living?" asked Malko.

"Maybe. James is going to give me another document where Lianin is identified by his real name. There might be a chance. So there you have it!"

She looked at her watch.

"If you want a quickie, now's the time. James is itching to see me, and since he's supposed to give me that document, I'm not about to stand him up."

Gwyneth certainly wasn't inhibited, thought Malko while paying the bill.

As they were leaving the Dorchester, she remarked:

"The information about the contract on Lianin is just a few days old, so we have to find him before the Russians can sanction him. Otherwise I'll have gone to a lot of trouble for nothing."

The moment they were in Malko's room, Gwyneth took off her suit jacket and pulled him close.

"It's nice to see you again," she said, sighing. "Too bad we don't have much time."

She had already started gently caressing him. For his part, he went to the most sensitive part of her body: the tips of her breasts. They were both feeling tense, but Malko felt his libido gradually waking up.

Leaning against a side table, Gwyneth raised her Chanel skirt, baring her long, stockinged legs. She gracefully pulled down her panties and drew Malko close. With almost no effort, he found himself deep inside her, held by the warm snugness of her cunt.

They made love deliberately, almost without speaking, until Malko suddenly lifted Gwyneth onto the table and thrust into her all the way, then came in a rush of pleasure.

Recess, unfortunately, was soon over.

After a quick trip to the bathroom, Gwyneth reappeared, impeccably dressed, a light dancing in her gray eyes.

"Wish me luck," she said with a touch of cynicism.

"You've already worked wonders!" he said.

Rem Tolkachev was mastering his fury, but with effort. The incident on Leningradsky Prospekt had caused a huge outcry, and the Russians were being abjectly apologetic over the three Americans' deaths.

He would have to ease off his pressure on Malko Linge, who was sure to be extremely well guarded now.

Besides, the problem could be solved in another way, Tolkachev realized. The man who knew too much was Arkady Lianin. He was the one to be eliminated.

That morning the spymaster had sent a note to the London *rezidentura* asking Lianin to contact him about an important, well-paid assignment in Moscow. Tolkachev wasn't kidding himself; Lianin was an old fox who knew what it meant when an agent was asked to "come home." But it was worth a try.

More important, Tolkachev contacted a Latvian gang with ties to the FSB whose members regularly used phony papers to get into England.

The group was the one that set the eight-hundred-thousand-dollar price on Lianin's head. The money would come from FSB coffers. That way there would be complete separation between the Russians and their victim. Lianin had often worked in Latvia, so there would be nothing surprising about the Latvian mafia bumping him off.

CHAPTER

21

Arkady Lianin opened his desk drawer first, then the secret compartment where he kept his Makarov. After pulling back the slide to check that a round was chambered, he put the semi-automatic in his leather briefcase.

"Valentina!" he called out, walking through the cottage. "I'm going to pick up the children!"

He got into his blue Mini and headed down the peaceful streets of Westminster Park, a quiet town southwest of London where everybody knew one another.

Lianin had arrived five years earlier, settled there by MI5. They had found him this house on a quiet street. His neighbors always said hello and didn't ask questions. Lianin spoke perfect English, so he blended in.

As he drove, he regularly glanced at his rearview mirror, checking for unfamiliar cars.

He reached the school early, so he took the time to drive around the block. Everything looked quiet. Other parents arrived, and Lianin picked up his own two children. He had slipped the semi-automatic between the front seats, just in case.

Suddenly a big Austin roared around the corner and Lianin's pulse quickened.

But it was just a neighbor who was running late.

Lianin drove back to the cottage, his mind elsewhere.

The last few years had passed peacefully. MI5 gave him some money, which allowed his family to live decently. Particularly since Lianin did an occasional job on the side.

But he was now cursing himself for accepting the offer of the man who called himself Pavel and had come especially from Moscow. Smiling and affable, Pavel—Lianin didn't know his real name—hadn't been threatening, exactly. But he knew all about Lianin's past and his various betrayals. Lianin had ditched the Estonian secret services, then the Russians, had briefly worked with the Americans, and finally accepted an offer from the Brits: a complete debriefing on all his past activities in exchange for a British passport and a driver's license. Plus a fair amount of money, though Lianin's needs were modest.

After a year of debriefing, the ex-FSB agent thought he was finally done with the secret world.

He hadn't heard from his former East European employers, and the British had assured him that if he didn't engage in any illegal activity, nothing would happen to him.

Then the man from Moscow had invited him to lunch at the elegant Fortnum & Mason tearoom on Piccadilly.

That was six months ago.

After chatting for a while, Pavel got to the point: his old Russian bosses needed his help in solving an awkward problem. Well aware that Estonian intelligence had hired Lianin to eliminate traitors, Pavel even dropped a few names into the conversation of ghosts that Lianin would have preferred to forget.

When the pastries came, the Moscow man explained specifically what he had in mind: a delicate FSB job to be carried out in England. It was right up Lianin's alley, he said.

An execution, something he had often done without any qualms, and for which he'd be paid a million dollars.

The offer was tempting. In England, Lianin was under very loose surveillance by MI5, which figured he was out to pasture. So he could take on a one-shot job, earn a million dollars, and go on living his quiet life.

Lianin asked the question:

"Who is the target?"

The Moscow man whispered, "Boris Berezovsky."

Lianin nearly fell off his chair.

"It can't be done! He's too well protected!"

Pavel set him straight.

"Berezovsky only has one bodyguard left," he said. "He lives alone in a big mansion in Ascot, in Surrey. The English are no longer interested in him. It's an easy job, and you'll be working with a first-class team."

Lianin knew that if the MI5 learned about it, he would not only lose everything he had in England, he would probably be kicked out of the country.

"It's impossible! If the Brits find out, I'm screwed."

"They won't find out," the Moscow man reassured him. "It'll only take a few days. But we need your skills."

"Besides," he added lightly, "if there's a problem, you can always come back to Moscow. You'd be given an interesting position in our organization. We value people like you, with experience."

But Lianin had no illusions. The "position" would be in either Lefortovo prison or in Siberia.

"I can't do it," he said firmly. "It's too dangerous."

Pavel had seemed annoyed, but no more than that. He paid the check and they parted on friendly terms. But he added meaningfully:

"You should think about it."

Nothing happened for the next few weeks. Then one day, as Lianin was picking up his children at school, he noticed a car that he'd never seen in the neighborhood before. There were two men in it, and it had a London license number.

Instinctively, he knew they were *siloviki*.

The men stayed in their car when the children came out. They followed Lianin when he drove off with his kids, then disappeared in traffic.

They came back every day for a week. He was tempted to talk to them, but didn't dare.

Then they disappeared.

Lianin thought the danger was past when he got a phone call.

"Arkady, this is your friend Pavel," said the man warmly. "I'm passing through London again. Want to have lunch at the same place?"

Lianin was too intimidated to refuse. He could have alerted MI5, of course, but that would have been as dangerous as grabbing a buzz saw with his bare hands.

He went to Fortnum & Mason.

This time the conversation was less relaxed. The Moscow man got right to the point.

"We need you, Arkady Vassilovich," he said. "You'll be doing a great service to Russia. The person behind this project is the most powerful man in the country, and your participation will earn his gratitude."

Vladimir Putin's gratitude wasn't a bad investment, but Lianin once again said no. Only this time he said it with his hands trembling and sweaty. He was clutching his quiet English life to his bosom.

And that's when Pavel's tone abruptly changed. He leaned across the table, his face close to Lianin's.

"You wouldn't want to live without your children, would you?"

he asked coldly. "You know what means we have at our disposal. Nothing and nobody can protect you."

As he spoke, he took some telephoto shots of Lianin's two children from his pocket and laid them on the table. Then his tone changed again.

"I'm sure I've convinced you!" he concluded affably. "You and I won't be meeting again. A man named Malinin will contact you soon with the operational details. You'll see; everything will go smoothly. Once the assignment is carried out, we'll send your fee wherever you like. And the English won't know a thing about it."

He got up and walked away, leaving the photos on the table. Caught in a trap, Lianin felt paralyzed. You couldn't fight the FSB, he knew. And he certainly didn't want his children run over by some anonymous hit-and-run driver.

Malinin showed up two weeks later. A poised man with a little goatee and glasses, he would never say what hotel he was staying at. They met several times in different places in London.

Malinin took Lianin to Surrey so he could become familiar with the estate where Berezovsky lived. Caught up in the operational details, Lianin slowly began to forget about the danger. He knew that MI5 was discreetly keeping an eye on him, but they hadn't made contact.

The two men made several reconnaissance trips. Gradually the project began to take shape.

One day, Malinin told him:

"Go have a drink at the Four Seasons Park Lane. A man will approach you and give you something."

"What?"

"Two vials of a certain substance. The second is a backup; you'll destroy it afterward."

Lianin met his contact at the Four Seasons, who handed him what looked like a cigar case and disappeared. The two men hardly spoke.

The Berezovsky killing took place the next day. It went off without a hitch, and the team members immediately left the country.

To Lianin's surprise, the oligarch's death made little impact in the press. It was as if he'd already been crossed off the list of the living.

A few days later, Lianin received a deposit receipt for a million dollars to a numbered account in Singapore that showed only the account number and a signature.

After that, life resumed as usual. With the mission accomplished, Lianin knew that his children were no longer in danger. He didn't hear from anybody. He stayed inside his home for several days, never going out.

He should have been in the clear.

With the children playing in the backseat, Lianin drove up to his gate and pressed the remote. The kids tumbled happily out of the car, and Lianin went into his office. He put the Makarov back in the drawer and sat down to smoke a cigarette.

A few days earlier he had received an "invitation" from the FSB *rezidentura*: an all-expenses-paid trip to the Russian capital. In other words, a one-way ticket to Lefortovo prison.

He had served his purpose, and they no longer needed him. He should have remembered the old Russian tradition: kill the killers. It made things easier.

And now he was stuck. Either he confessed everything to MI5, or he fought the FSB alone, with no chance of winning.

His cell phone rang and he looked at the screen: an unknown Latvian number.

The voice was unknown as well, though warm and friendly.

"It's your old pal Stanislaw! I wanted to tell you that some people you know are flying to London. I think they'd like to see you. Do you remember Laukas?"

Lianin did: a vicious Latvian gangster with ties to the FSB.

He felt his stomach tighten. This time, it was all over. They were sending a team to kill him.

CHAPTER

22

"Do you think we should tell the Brits what's happening?"
asked Malko. "We have enough information to go on."

Stanley Dexter had invited Malko to the embassy for a breakfast meeting. Since they'd learned Arkady Lianin's false identity thanks to Gwyneth Robertson, their investigation had taken a big step forward. But they were now at an impasse.

Without knowing the city where "Mr. Touria" lived, there was no way to find his telephone number. His address, 111 Newham Way, posed the same problem. It occurred in hundreds of English towns, and there was no way to sift through them all.

The CIA station chief wasn't enthusiastic about bringing the British aboard.

"I wouldn't," he said. "First, they'd be angry that we learned they're sheltering an ex-KGB agent in the country. There's nothing shocking about that, but it's one of those little secrets that you don't want to get out. Second, we would have to tell them what we've learned about Lianin's past."

"Don't you think they know?" asked Malko.

"No, I don't. MI5 would never authorize an operation that involved them in the Berezovsky murder. That's too serious. I suspect they don't know about any of it. If we tell them, we'd be putting them in an impossible situation, and they'd resent us for it."

"In that case, we're stuck."

There was no way to follow the trail any further.

"I think Lianin's probably going to stay in England and lie low," said Dexter. "It's the only place where he's safe. He probably figures things will eventually settle down."

A hush descended on the two men. It felt depressing.

I may have risked my life in Moscow and London for nothing, Malko thought gloomily. Aloud, he said:

"Very well. I'm due to see Gwyneth again. Maybe she'll have something new."

"If she hasn't, you can just write up that report for Langley and fly back to your castle," said the station chief. "Let's check in with each other again tomorrow."

Taking a flashlight, Arkady Lianin told his wife that he was going for a walk. He opened the gate to his little yard and stepped into the quiet street, with the Makarov slipped into his belt.

He walked around the houses next to his and checked several nearby streets without noticing anything suspicious. A couple of times he heard a noise and whirled around, but it was only the wind. He took his Latvian friend's warning very seriously. A number of gangs worked with the FSB, and they weren't above doing the occasional favor.

Besides, killing Lianin would be easy. Aside from the Makarov, he had no way to defend himself. And he knew the people he might be dealing with were cold-blooded killers. They would casually fly into England, get weapons from local accomplices, and come shoot or stab him.

What could he do?

Tell the local police that he'd been threatened? That would immediately get back to MI5, which would ask for an explanation he'd be forced to give. His dread was that the British might send him into outer darkness, where his life expectancy would be practically zero.

Lianin returned to the cottage and went into his study. His wife was already asleep. He sat down at his desk, poured himself a shot of scotch, and gulped it down.

He'd been racking his brains but couldn't think of a way out, short of putting a bullet in his head. And that wasn't his style.

To think that after all his many double crosses he had finally carved out a peaceful life for himself!

Two hours later, he was no further along in his thinking.

He again went out into the yard to admire his rosebushes. He was now carrying the Makarov everywhere.

He bitterly cursed the FSB and its ironclad rule: liquidate assassins once they've done their job. Lianin knew the rule, of course. He just never thought it would apply to him.

Gwyneth's face was drawn and she had circles under her gray eyes, but those eyes were alight with joy. Malko had a feeling that she hadn't been wasting her time. They'd met in the Promenade at the Dorchester, and Gwyneth was wolfing down some little sandwiches she'd ordered.

"I got up at seven, and I've had meetings all day long," she moaned. "I'm dead on my feet."

"Did you see your boyfriend again?"

She nodded.

"We're practically married!" she said with an ambiguous smile. "And James outdid himself. Here!"

She took a sheet of paper from her briefcase and handed it to Malko. Written on *Sunday Times* stationery, it was a letter of recommendation for Lianin, who had apparently worked on two assignments for the great English weekly.

The first was an investigation into a ring that supplied phony passports to phony Russian immigrants, some of whom were connected to the intelligence services. The second had to do with students who used fake documents to create business visas for themselves.

The letter stressed that Mr. Lianin had carried out these investigations at great personal risk, as he was dealing with dangerous criminals from Eastern Europe. The warm recommendation was signed *Nick Fielding, Senior Reporter.*

Malko handed the letter back to Gwyneth.

"This is interesting, but it doesn't tell us where Lianin is living," he said, feeling a little disappointed. "We'll have to talk to this Fielding fellow."

"That won't be easy," said Gwyneth. "He moved to Australia three years ago. But I have the name of the man who replaced him: Luke Harding."

Malko shrugged.

"I'd be surprised if he cooperated with the CIA," he said. "British journalists don't do that sort of thing. And this letter doesn't get us anywhere."

"You didn't examine it carefully enough," she said. "Look at the top left, above the date."

When Malko leaned closer, he could make out some very faint marks, partly erased. All numbers.

"I'll bet dollars to donuts that's Lianin's phone number," Gwyneth continued. "After all, Fielding must have had a way to reach him."

Malko's pulse picked up.

"Do you think so?"

"I'm almost positive. The trick now is to figure out the numbers. With grazing light, we ought to be able to see them."

"Supposing you're right, what do we do then?"

"We set a trap!" she said eagerly. "Draw Lianin into our net. Offer him a well-paid investigative job and arrange a meeting."

Malko's brain was getting back up to speed.

"That might take quite some time," he said, "but if this really is his phone number, we've got a chance. We need to find somebody in the Agency who can play the role of the reporter. Somebody with an English accent."

"That should be possible," said Gwyneth.

Malko was feeling hopeful again.

"When do you think you'll have figured the number out?"

"By tomorrow morning."

"Can you come to the station?"

"I'll swing by on my way to work. And if I'm missing a number, you can try variations."

At last, they might have a way of locating the ex-KGB agent! Lianin had to answer the phone, of course, and also be willing to work for the *Sunday Times* again. But it could turn out to be a giant step.

The Latvians had arrived!

As Lianin drove his children to class, he spotted a rental car that followed him to the school, and then disappeared. There were two Slavic-looking men inside, who didn't even glance at him. They had started their reconnaissance. It could take a while. They were in no hurry, but the countdown had begun.

Lianin drove home, his mind in a whirl.

Now his back was really to the wall. If he didn't take action, he was a dead man. He could save his family by offering himself up to the killers, he knew. They were vicious, but they weren't crazy. They had a contract for eight hundred thousand dollars to kill him, and they wouldn't care about anything else.

Lianin went into his study, took out a little address book, and found the emergency number MI5 had given him. He'd been told the number was answered twenty-four hours a day.

He slowly dialed it, then abruptly hung up, hoping that his own number hadn't registered at the other end. If he sounded the alarm, MI5 would certainly keep him from being killed, but what would happen after that?

He would lose everything and be deported. And he had nothing to offer in exchange, no way to strike a deal.

Lianin was still thinking when his landline rang, which didn't happen often.

He picked it up and said, "Hello?"

There was no answer, just the sound of regular breathing. It wasn't a wrong number. It was the beginning of the pressure.

Lianin sat slumped in an armchair, unable to think.

He felt like an animal at bay.

He again briefly thought of shooting himself, to solve his problems.

Then he went back outside, studying the quiet streets of his suburban neighborhood. A neighbor doing her shopping called out a friendly greeting.

"And how are we today, Mr. Touria?"

"Very well, thanks," said the Russian. He went back inside his house, the place where he felt safest—but for how much longer?

Malko had already explained the situation to Dexter when a smiling Gwyneth Robertson came in.

"Were you able to figure out the number?" asked Malko.

"I have three possibles," she said. "There's one digit I can't make out. I can't tell if it's a five, an eight, or a zero. You'll just have to try them!"

"Get the right one, and we'll have Lianin on the line," said Malko. "But we'll only get one chance to make the sale."

"I have to run," Gwyneth called over her shoulder as she left the office. "Good luck!"

"We have a Brit who works at the embassy who's willing to help us," Dexter announced. "His name's John Cavendish. He's a Cockney and as clever as a fox."

"Can you have him come up?"

Cavendish walked in ten minutes later. A husky redhead with blue eyes and a lively manner, he was delighted to be part of the operation.

"I've already briefed John, and he knows what to say," the station chief explained. "He'll be Luke Harding, a reporter at the *Sunday Times*. He's taken over for Nick Fielding and needs a good investigator for an investigative article about Baltic networks inside Great Britain."

"The question of money is important," Malko stressed. "Be sure to mention it right away."

Cavendish nodded.

"I plan to offer him ten thousand quid, plus expenses," he said. "That's a lot of dosh."

The three men exchanged a last look, and Malko gave the signal.

Cavendish sat down at the station chief's desk, put the telephone on speaker, and carefully dialed the first number, 7334 823 273.

A woman picked up on the third ring. Cavendish introduced himself as Luke Harding and asked to speak to Mr. Arkady Lianin.

"I don't know the gentleman," she said shortly. "You've dialed the wrong number."

She hung up.

They tried the next number. It was so quiet in the office, you could hear a pin drop. The phone rang and rang in emptiness somewhere. At the fifteenth ring, Cavendish hung up.

"Let's try the third one," suggested Malko.

The tension had gone up a notch. As carefully as he had before, Cavendish dialed the final number. It was answered on the third ring.

"I'd like to speak to Arkady Lianin," Cavendish said.

"Who's calling?" asked a deep bass voice.

"My name's Luke Harding, and I'm a reporter for the *Sunday Times*," he said. "A Mr. Lianin worked for my colleague Nick Fielding a couple of times, and Nicky gave me this number. He's moved to Australia, and I've taken over his job. I've got an assignment: investigating criminal gangs from Eastern Europe in Britain. It's risky, but very well paid.

"This is Arkady Lianin, isn't it?"

"Yes, it is."

CHAPTER

23

The three men in the CIA office held their breath during the tense silence that followed. Then Cavendish continued, still in his Luke Harding persona.

"Mr. Lianin, Nicky had good things to say about you, so I'll be brief. I need an investigator like you for an in-depth assignment. Can we get together to talk about it?"

The silence—in which you could hear even a very, *very* small pin drop—was finally broken by Lianin.

"I don't think I'm interested," he said in his deep voice. "I don't need money. But thank you."

They were all sure he was going to hang up. Before he could, Cavendish jumped into the breach.

"Mr. Lianin, we can meet without your having to commit. This is a major gig, and very well paid. We're offering a fee of ten thousand pounds. And you're the perfect person for the job. May I come see you?"

This time the answer came like a shot.

"No! Nobody comes to my place!"

"In that case, we can meet wherever you like," said Cavendish quickly. "In a café or a restaurant, say. There's a very nice place on Virginia Street near the paper."

"I don't like restaurants."

Cavendish laughed.

"In that case, you can pick the place," he said.

Another silence fell. To the people in the office, it felt interminable. Finally, Lianin slowly said:

"Tomorrow at noon, under Wellington Arch near Hyde Park."

Before Cavendish could say anything, the Russian hung up.

The tension in the room abruptly evaporated.

"Bingo!" shouted Stanley Dexter. "Well done, John! And Malko, please give Gwyneth a big thank-you for me.

"We're going to need a hell of a setup, to be able to follow Lianin after the meeting. For the moment, all we have is his cell phone. I'll wire Langley."

"Do you think they'll commit the resources?"

Dexter gave him a fierce look.

"They damn well better! First of all, they're the ones who asked me to investigate the Berezovsky affair. And second, Lianin tried to kill you, and you're one of the Agency's most valuable assets. Besides, if we can assemble a complete dossier on Berezovsky, we'll have something to hold over our MI5 friends' heads if they ever behave badly some day. We're a team of rivals, after all."

"Okay, rendezvous here at eleven o'clock tomorrow," said Dexter. "And keep your fingers crossed."

Malko was anxious for the next day to dawn.

Lianin hung up feeling thoughtful. The timing of the *Sunday Times* offer couldn't be better, assuming they were serious. Ten thousand pounds would let him fly to New Zealand for a couple of weeks, where he had service friends. It would take the pressure off, because the Latvian killers couldn't hang around London forever. He knew they wouldn't go after his family, so he could leave with his mind at ease.

Afterward . . . well, that would be another story. Maybe he

could ask MI5 to relocate him. The FSB knew only his current address.

A sudden thought occurred to him. How would this Luke Harding person recognize him? But he didn't worry for long; Nick had probably left him some photos.

Lianin had chosen Wellington Arch because from there you could walk into Hyde Park. Long experience had left him distrustful of places where he could be overheard.

He went out for another surveillance drive, taking his Makarov. Getting shot and killed now would be too stupid.

Arkady Lianin was feeling a surge of new energy.

Malko took Gwyneth to a Piccadilly brasserie to celebrate their breakthrough, and she was looking radiant.

"God, I hope Lianin comes to the meeting," she said. "After that, it'll be a piece of cake."

"The Agency is going whole hog," Malko assured her. "A dozen case officers will be on the stakeout. We absolutely have to find out where Lianin lives. But once we do, we'll have the upper hand."

The young woman raised her champagne glass to their success.

"And I'll gradually get my life and my freedom back. I think it's proof of how much I like you that I've done what I did."

Malko smiled at her.

"Oh, come on, Gwyn, it wasn't such a chore! You like the man!"

"For a quick fling, sure, but what I've been doing is different. James thinks I'm in love with him and I let him believe it. But in fact, I'm manipulating him—for you. It's going to come as a terrible shock for him.

"It might be time for me to take a little trip to the States and give him the bad news when I come back. Or else send him a Dear John letter. I don't want to hurt him."

"But that was your job, before, to mix your work life with your personal life," Malko pointed out.

"Yeah, and I thought I'd finished with all that. Now I'm an honest analyst and finally earning a decent living. I'll probably get married and have kids one of these days."

There was a hint of wistfulness in her voice.

Malko put his hand on hers.

"Gwyneth, I don't think I'll ever be able to thank you enough. It was your work that got us this far."

She gave a slightly forced laugh.

"Then pour me some more champagne and let's have fun this evening. I'm free as a bird. James is having dinner with his mother."

John Cavendish had been pacing under the Wellington Arch for ten minutes when he saw a tall man walking up Apsley Way toward him. He was wearing a blue canvas jacket and gray pants and carried a little shoulder bag. Having seen old photographs, Cavendish immediately recognized it was Arkady Lianin.

He rushed over to him with a big smile and stuck out his hand.

"Mr. Lianin? I'm Luke Harding; we talked on the phone. I'm glad you were able to come."

With his shaved head, heavy eyebrows, and protruding ears, Lianin was an intimidating figure. He looked Cavendish up and down, and asked:

"How do I know you're really with the *Sunday Times*?"

"That's easy, here!"

From his wallet Cavendish took a *Times* press ID and a business card, both in the name of Luke Harding, and handed them over.

Little masterpieces created by the CIA's Technical Division.

Lianin studied the cards quickly and gave them back.

"Want to have a drink somewhere, so we can talk?" asked Cavendish. "We could go to the Hilton, the Four Seasons, the Lanesborough . . ."

The Russian shook his head.

"No. We're going to walk in Hyde Park."

He was being cautious, and Cavendish didn't argue.

"You're right, walking's very healthy. Let's go."

Anyway, half the CIA case officers were in the vicinity, on foot, in cars, and on motorcycles, and all connected by radio: a web Lianin wouldn't be able to escape.

Walking ahead of Cavendish, he crossed the square and took the Knightsbridge underground passage near the Lanesborough.

They entered the park near Apsley House and walked on the path known as Lovers' Walk along with a mixed crowd of families, regular strollers, and a few horseback riders.

Lianin seemed to relax in the bucolic environment.

"So why did you want to meet with me, exactly?" he asked.

"Nick was very impressed by your investigation of the Russian mob in London four years ago," said Cavendish. "I'd like to take the same topic and bring it up to date, if you can gather the facts."

"It can be done, but it's dangerous," said Lianin. "Last time, I had killers after me, and I almost didn't make it out alive."

"I know you're a brave man," said Cavendish. "Have you heard of any developments since then?"

Lianin paused, seeming to think.

"Yes, I have. There's a new gang of Latvians who are working with the Russian FSB. They specialize in forgeries, executions, and extortion. But investigating them is difficult. I can infiltrate them, but it will take time."

Cavendish brushed the objection aside.

"No problem. When could you start?"

Lianin gave him a cool glance.

"As soon as we agree on the conditions."

"As I said on the phone, we're prepared to pay ten thousand pounds plus expenses."

The Russian shook his head.

"That's not enough. The job's too dangerous. I want ten thousand pounds on signing, and the same when we're finished."

"That's a hell of a lot of money!" cried Cavendish. "And it's a decision I can't make on my own. I'll have to talk to my editor. Naturally, I'll push the request as hard as I can."

He paused.

"Can we meet again tomorrow—same time, same place?"

"The time's okay," said the Russian, "but I'll phone you to set the place."

They had walked about five hundred yards along Lovers' Walk and now turned back toward where they had entered the park. When they reached Knightsbridge, Lianin put out his hand to shake.

"See you tomorrow," he said. "I'll call at eleven."

He crossed the sidewalk and headed for the Hyde Park Corner underground station.

A few moments later, Cavendish's radio crackled.

"Mr. Blue here. I've got him. He's going down into the Tube."

Malko and Dexter were waiting in an unmarked car parked just beyond the Lanesborough. The CIA station chief was connected to all the case officers by radio. He turned to Malko, and said:

"He just got off at the West Brompton station and is walking west."

"You have people out there?" asked Malko.

"Yes. Mr. White is driving down Brompton Road, and Mr. Red is approaching on a motorcycle."

After a few minutes of radio silence, a new call came in:

"The 'customer' just picked up his car in a car park and is driving off. A blue Austin Mini, license plate 538BGD. We are maintaining contact. He's heading west and seems to be going home."

"Roger that," said Dexter. "We'll follow at a safe distance."

He turned to Malko with a big grin.

"I think we're about to hit the jackpot!"

The car parked at the start of Newham Way had been rented under a false name with false papers. Two men were sitting in front. A Skorpion submachine gun lay on the floor next to the man in back.

The three Latvians had decided to hit Lianin when he was coming home. Early afternoon was the perfect time: the streets were empty. They would shoot him while he was parking his Mini and leave in a series of getaway cars.

In two hours they would be in London, where they would split up and leave England by separate routes.

Having earned eight hundred thousand dollars.

Suddenly the man behind the wheel hissed:

"There he is!"

The blue Austin had just turned onto Newham Way and was coming toward them.

The Latvian started the rental car. Their plan was simple: pull up next to the Austin and shoot the driver before he could get out.

The rental eased away from the sidewalk and slowly headed for Lianin's car.

Mark Spencer and John Taylor, the case officers who had followed Lianin to his Winchester Park suburb, relaxed a little as they saw the Austin Mini pull over in front of a cottage. At last, they knew where the former KGB agent lived.

They would drive by, note the address, and keep going.

But suddenly Taylor noticed a car coming the other way. Instead of going on, it stopped next to the Austin, whose driver was still inside.

A man got out of the back holding a big submachine gun and walked toward the Austin.

"Holy shit!" exclaimed Spencer. He leaped out of the car, ripped the Colt 3 from his ankle holster, and chambered a round.

The man with the submachine gun saw him at the same moment and stopped dead. After a few seconds' hesitation, the astonished killer jumped into his car, which then roared past the CIA Ford, turned onto the next street, and disappeared.

Spencer got back into his own car and drove on. John Taylor was already talking on the radio, describing the unexpected event.

"Stay in the zone!" ordered Dexter. "Protect the customer!"

Lianin had seen the whole thing. The man with the Skorpion was obviously one of the Latvian killers sent by the FSB. But who was the other armed man, whose intervention had saved his life?

He didn't seem to be with MI5.

Hands shaking, Lianin slammed the car door and sprinted for his house. He was terrified that he would stumble across the dead bodies of his family. But when he opened the door, his wife called to him.

"Is that you, dear?"

"Yes, I'm home," he said, hurrying into his study. His legs were wobbly and his head was spinning. He took a gulp of whiskey.

Without that miraculous intervention, he'd be a dead man. He would never have had time to draw his Makarov.

Lianin closed his eyes: it was high time he got out of London.

On the fourth floor of the American embassy, a council of war was under way.

A puzzled Stanley Dexter had just summed up the Newham Way incident.

"This is a hell of a new development! Who's trying to kill Lianin?"

"I think I know," said Malko. "My investigation in Moscow alerted the FSB. I bet they got scared that we would track Lianin down, so they decided to kill him. Liquidating assassins is an old Soviet habit, as you know."

"This changes the stakes," said Dexter. "Maybe it's time to warn the Brits."

"Why should we?" exclaimed Malko. "We have a huge advantage now. We've located Lianin, and we also know that he's in danger. This would be the perfect time to offer him a deal."

"What kind of deal?"

"That will depend on the United States," said Malko. "Right now, besides the stick, we have a carrot: we can protect him. Is the Agency prepared to get involved?"

"What would the deal be?" asked the station chief.

"A complete confession in exchange for extended witness protection; maybe resettlement in the United States. If Lianin feels threatened, he might agree."

"I'll call Langley right away," said Dexter. "Who's going to offer him the deal?"

"If it's okay with you, I will," Malko said with a thin smile. "I have an advantage: Lianin knows me. After all, he tried to kill me."

CHAPTER

24

After making sure the front door didn't have a peephole, Malko rang the bell at Arkady Lianin's cottage. It was eleven in the morning and the Russian's car was parked on the street, so he had to be at home.

The door's abrupt opening took Malko by surprise, because he hadn't heard any noise inside.

There stood Lianin in a T-shirt and khaki pants, staring at him in astonishment. He went to close the door, but Malko had already stuck his foot in the opening. In Russian, he said:

"Gospodin Lianin, I have no bad intentions toward you. And I hope you don't have any, either. I'm not armed, but the two gentlemen behind me are."

Malko, who was wearing a Kevlar bulletproof vest under his jacket, pointed to the two CIA officers behind him, who had been watching the cottage since the night before. They had Beretta 92s in shoulder holsters.

"I'd like to come in, if you don't mind."

Clearly overwhelmed, Lianin silently stepped aside to let Malko pass. It was cool in the cottage. The two case officers followed, and they all went into Lianin's study.

The Russian dropped into an armchair and waved Malko to its mate. The two Americans sat down.

When he was seated, Lianin finally found his voice.

"What do you want?" he asked in his low bass.

"To make you an offer you can't refuse," Malko answered. "It's in your interest. I now know the exact role you played in the assassination of Boris Berezovsky. I conducted a long investigation in Moscow. I even know the name of the person who gave you the substance you used to poison him: Ilya Sokolov, a *Forbes Russia* journalist who also works with the FSB. And many other details besides.

"Yesterday I learned that people are trying to kill you, and that has changed my approach. I think I know what's involved, but I want to hear it from your own mouth. Who wants to get rid of you?"

After a pause, Lianin croaked:

"The FSB."

"Why?"

"They want me to return to Russia, to liquidate me. I refused, so they're trying to kill me here."

"Yet you've served them faithfully. The Berezovsky operation was a success."

The Russian looked at him with a touch of contempt.

"You don't know them!" he snapped. "I'm a security risk. If I were arrested, I might talk. They must avoid that at any cost. It's standard procedure in the Service. But you never think it'll apply to you."

Lianin sounded bitter, but Malko wasn't inclined to pity him.

"Were those men trying to kill you Russians?"

"No, they're Latvian gangsters who work with the FSB. Very dangerous guys."

"Do you think you'll be able to escape them?"

"No, I don't," said Lianin, shaking his head slowly. "Not in the long run."

He paused, then said:

"I'd like to know how you found me."

Malko smiled.

"The *Sunday Times* man you saw yesterday is with the CIA," he said. "It was all a setup. In the beginning, we thought we'd just park you in a safe house and tell MI5 the whole story, to neutralize you. The fact that you're in serious danger changes things, and we may have a better solution. Better for you, and better for us."

"What's that?"

"We're not trying to avenge Boris Berezovsky's death. What we want is to assemble a dossier on the affair that we can use against the Russians. I suspect that if you didn't have a price on your head, you wouldn't cooperate. But things are different now. You want to get out of this alive, and we can help."

"I don't see what you're after," said Lianin, "since you say you know all about the case."

"We want a detailed confession of your role in killing Berezovsky, with all the involvement of the FSB acting at the behest of the Russian government. When you sign a statement like that, you'll be in our hands, of course.

"You can also refuse. In that case, we'll withdraw and stop protecting you. But your life expectancy will be extremely short, I'm afraid."

Lianin rubbed his face and his shaved head. He looked haggard.

"Will you tell MI5 about this?"

"We haven't decided yet. We might not have to. Anyway, do you intend to stay in England?"

"I don't know," said the Russian, shaking his head, still in shock. "I didn't sleep last night, and I don't know if I'm coming or going. But I don't trust the Americans. They've let me down in the past."

"You don't have any choice," said Malko. "But it's not in our interest to sell you out. What we want is a detailed, signed confession that implicates the FSB."

"If I say yes, what happens then?" asked Lianin in an unexpectedly weak voice.

"The Agency will protect you around the clock for as long as you stay here. It will be invisible, but nobody will be able to harm you. After you've done what we want, you'll have the choice of several witness protection programs, here or abroad."

"Would that include my family?"

"Absolutely."

Malko looked at his watch.

"I'm waiting for your answer."

Lianin bent his head for a few moments, then raised it and looked at Malko darkly.

In a weary voice, he said, "I accept."

Malko felt he'd aged a decade from the nervous tension. The CIA group had returned to Grosvenor Square with Lianin a half hour earlier. Two case officers stayed behind at the cottage to guard his wife and children.

Dexter ordered sandwiches, coffee, and bottled water sent up from the cafeteria, and he and Malko were having a snack in his office.

Two rooms down the hall, a pair of Russian-speaking operatives had started Lianin's debriefing. Everything was being filmed and recorded.

"I would never have thought this business would end so well," said Dexter, grinning at Malko. "With the material Lianin gives us, we'll be able to play Putin like a sock puppet. His goal was to never have the Russian state connected to Berezovsky's death as a matter of prestige. Well, tough luck, tovarich!"

"You should thank Gwyneth Robertson," said Malko. "Without the *Sunday Times* trick, we would never have gotten to Lianin."

"Incidentally," said Dexter, "I just got some bad news from Moscow."

"What's that?"

"Irina Lopukin died, apparently of a heart attack. It was in the newspapers."

Another victim of collateral damage.

"They took their revenge on her," said Malko, feeling troubled. He had caused her death, he knew. "I'll have flowers put on her grave. She was very helpful."

And part of a ragtag gang that had somehow defeated the terrifying FSB and Kremlin machine.

Dexter's telephone rang. He listened for a moment, then turned to Malko.

"It's the debriefers. They're getting to the Berezovsky killing. Want to watch it live?"

"Of course!"

Arkady Lianin looked as if he'd lost fifteen pounds. He didn't even glance up when the two men entered the room and silently sat down behind him.

In a calm voice, one of the interrogators asked:

"Gospodin Lianin, what happened on the morning of March 23, 2013?"

The Russian answered in a monotone:

"I set up surveillance around the estate where Boris Berezovsky had arrived with his bodyguard Uri Dan the night before. We were sure he'd slept there. From the listening devices we'd placed inside, we knew Dan would be going to London for a couple of hours, leaving Berezovsky alone."

"How many men did you have?"

"Five, plus me. I already gave you their names. The bodyguard drove off, and we followed him to make sure he didn't turn around and come back. We neutralized the estate's security system, then entered the gate and went into the house.

"We didn't see anybody.

"We knew the layout of the house, so it was easy to find Berezovsky's bedroom. He was stretched out on his bed, reading. He was dressed.

"As soon as he saw us, he went for a gun in his night table but didn't have time to get it. Pavel and Oleg immobilized him with a headlock. Then Oleg gave him an injection of the substance I gave you. The two of them held him down. He struggled a little, but the poison acted very quickly and he passed out."

"Was somebody outside, watching the house?"

"Yes, of course.

"When Berezovsky was unconscious, we dragged him into the bathroom. Oleg tied a rope to the showerhead and tied the other end around his neck. The hardest part was lifting him up, because he was quite heavy."

"Was he still alive?" asked the agent.

"Yes. But that's when we had a problem. He slipped out of our arms and fell to the floor, snapping the cord tied around the showerhead. We didn't have time to try again. We left the way we came, and restarted the security system. We were in London half an hour later."

Lianin fell silent, then said:

"Can I have a cigarette?"

Malko and Dexter stepped out of the room.

"When this report is complete, can I ask you a favor, Stanley?"

"Sure! What would you like?"

"Send a copy to Moscow in the diplomatic pouch," said Malko. "And see that it gets to Vladimir Putin personally. It should keep him awake nights for a good long time."

About the Translator

William Rodarmor (1942–) is a French literary translator of some forty books. Before *Revenge of the Kremlin*, he translated two other Malko Linge thrillers for Vintage, *The Madmen of Benghazi* and *Chaos in Kabul*. He has won the Lewis Galantière Award from the American Translators Association and worked as a contract interpreter for the U.S. State Department.

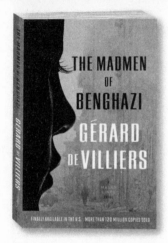
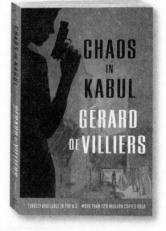